A woman alone in the dark with a stranger...

Hands in the air. Feet wide apart. She was prepared to fight if the need arose. She'd had nearly identical training as the federal agent cohorts she once worked with, but she wasn't even close to the stranger's level. His gaze skimmed her body. The formfitting T-shirt and jeans didn't leave any room for concealing a weapon.

She certainly didn't look like his idea of a private detective. But looks were often deceiving. After all, he was an expert at creating illusions. Perhaps *she* was an illusion designed to do exactly what she appeared to be trying to do: drawing him into a trap.

DEBRA
WEBB

GUARDIAN ANGEL

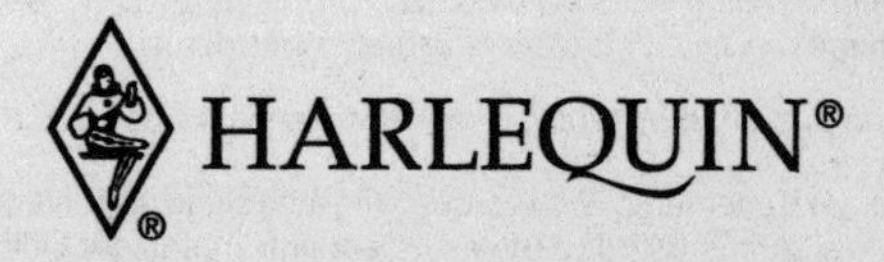

TORONTO • NEW YORK • LONDON
AMSTERDAM • PARIS • SYDNEY • HAMBURG
STOCKHOLM • ATHENS • TOKYO • MILAN • MADRID
PRAGUE • WARSAW • BUDAPEST • AUCKLAND

To all members of law enforcement, local, federal or international, the true guardian angels who protect our children.

ISBN-13: 978-0-373-69309-2
ISBN-10: 0-373-69309-5

GUARDIAN ANGEL

This edition published by arrangement with Harlequin Books S.A.

www.eHarlequin.com

Printed in U.S.A.

ABOUT THE AUTHOR

Debra Webb was born in Scottsboro, Alabama, to parents who taught her that anything is possible if you want it bad enough. She began writing at age nine. Eventually, she met and married the man of her dreams, and tried various occupations, including selling vacuum cleaners and working in a factory, a daycare center, a hospital and a department store. When her husband joined the military, they moved to Berlin, Germany, and Debra became a secretary in the commanding general's office. By 1985 they were back in the States, and they finally moved to Tennessee, to a small town where everyone knows everyone else. With the support of her husband and two beautiful daughters, Debra took up writing again, looking to mystery and movies for inspiration. In 1998 her dream of writing for Harlequin Books came true. You can write to Debra at P.O. Box 64, Huntland, Tennessee 37345, or visit her Web site at www.debrawebb.com to find out exciting news about her next book.

Books by Debra Webb

HARLEQUIN INTRIGUE

891—PERSON OF INTEREST
909—INVESTIGATING 101*
916—RAW TALENT*
934—THE HIDDEN HEIR *
951—A COLBY CHRISTMAS*
983—A SOLDIER'S OATH**
989—HOSTAGE SITUATION**
995—COLBY VS. COLBY**
1023—COLBY REBUILT*
1042—GUARDIAN ANGEL*

*Colby Agency
**The Equalizers

CAST OF CHARACTERS

Guardian Angel—Is he really a savior or merely a vigilante? And what of his alter ego, Nathan Tyler, the mysterious recluse with far too many secrets of his own?

Ann Linker Martin—A Colby Agency investigator with a deep, dark secret of her own. Will that secret prevent her from doing her job?

Victoria Colby-Camp—The head of the Colby Agency. Victoria has complete faith in all her investigators. She is certain that Ann will not fail her or the client.

Katherine Fowler—A mother who will go to any and all lengths to find her missing child.

Trey Fowler—The child's father is terrified that the Colby Agency's involvement will jeopardize his child's life.

Kevin Addison—The top public relations agent in the business. How far will he go to put his boss in the limelight?

Owen Johnson—Will loyalty and ambition continue to outweigh any sense of basic human compassion he has left?

Phillip Kendall—Wealth and power are the only moral codes he follows.

Ian Michaels and Simon Ruhl—The top men at the Colby Agency.

Chapter One

Western Virginia
Monday 8:35 p.m.

The girl was here.

He could feel it, could taste the evil in the air. His senses went on high alert.

Moving silently, he eased closer to the rundown shack that sat deep in the wilderness backing up against the George Washington National Forest.

An acrid chemical stench lingered in the September air. He recognized that solvent-laden stink. The remote setting provided the perfect anonymous spot. Most meth labs were found in trailer homes, old sheds, run-down motels and places exactly like this, where no one wanted to look.

It was too dark to see just now, but somewhere nearby there would be a mounting refuse pile that would tell the tale and would, all by itself, provide sufficient probable cause for a search warrant. But he wasn't here about the classic lowlife-style meth lab.

He was here for the girl.

His heart rate remaining stable despite the anticipation coursing in his veins, he stole toward the east side of the shack. Light poured through the bottom portion of the single window on that end, its faint glow cutting through the darkness like a ray of hope.

Anticipation fueled his determination, simultaneously limiting his patience; but before going in, he needed the number and location of the trouble he would encounter inside. He pulled the bill of the cap lower over his face and prepared to move closer.

The front door swung open and a lone man, maybe six feet, one-thirty or one-forty pounds, lumbered onto the ramshackle porch. He muttered what might have been song lyrics as he stumbled down the steps. Dark hair. Ragged jeans, T-shirt sporting what appeared to be the logo of some defunct heavy metal band. Not enough light reached beyond the door to determine whether or not he was carrying anything other than the sheathed knife on his belt.

The skinny degenerate lurched his way to the tree line and proceeded to relieve himself against the bark of the closest one. Too bad he'd chosen east over west. Probably didn't know one from the other.

Less than five seconds were necessary to acquire his position. The silenced end of the weapon's muzzle landed against the back of his skull, and the biological urge that had brought the scumbag to the tree halted.

"What the—"

"Don't move."

"Who the hell do you think you are?" the man sneered. "Five-oh?" The metal-on-metal grate of his fly closing punctuated the cocky questions.

Grabbing a handful of the scumbag's hair, he jerked his no-good head back and jammed the muzzle against his temple. "No one you want to know, trust me."

The fool had the poor judgment to laugh. "Unless you've got some big-time backup, you're a dead man—that's who you are." He tried to twist free, went for his knife. But he wasn't nearly fast enough.

Unlucky for him.

One snap of his useless neck and he slumped to the ground. Another clump of meaningless

DNA. From the smell of him and his clothes, he was hazardous waste anyway.

Acting quickly would be vital now. The dead man's associates would be looking for their compadre if he didn't come back inside in a timely manner.

Focusing on slowing his respiration and calming his pulse, he zeroed in on that one window on the east end of the shack that had been left partially uncovered. Without a single sound that might give him away, he stole into position. The exposed window was most likely an attempt at increased airflow. An unindustrious method of venting the dangerous chemical gases the illegal work inside produced.

The front portion of the shack appeared to be one rectangular room. A tattered couch and chair claimed the floor space closest to the open window. Beyond the sitting area was a makeshift kitchen. Piles of lithium batteries, hundreds of boxes of what was probably a popular allergy relief medication or one of its clones littered a table. A pistol—a .32 maybe—lay in plain sight.

A heavyset woman who looked to be about thirty monitored her latest concoction, a cigarette dangling from the corner of her mouth. The *cook*. The dead guy was probably the *shop-*

per. Lots of supplies lying around. Too much so to be just a feed-my-habit operation. These dirtbags were manufacturing with the intent to sell.

Rage tore through him at the idea that kidnapping had been added to their sick MO, obliterating the much-needed calm. He tamped down the rage, refocused on what he'd come here to do.

Get the girl.

That meant going inside.

The cook wore an MP3 player clipped to the waistband of her jeans, wires extended up to the buds in her ears. Several inches of dark growth revealed the true color of her stringy blond hair. She sang along with the tune playing in the mini headphones, belting out the words in rusty harmony.

He listened but couldn't make out any other sound. Just the woman's unpleasant off-key lyrics and the squeak of the floor beneath her exaggerated dance moves as she went about her dirty business.

No sign of the girl.

But she was here.

He could feel it.

He'd never been wrong. He wouldn't be wrong this time.

There was at least one room other than this one. A door near the couch offered access. A bedroom, probably. And the most likely place to stash a hostage.

Fury contracted in his muscles despite his having banished it only moments ago. He kicked it aside again. Emotion had no place in what he was about to do.

Deciding to use the dead man as his invitation, he returned to the scumbag's location and hefted him onto his shoulder, then headed to the front door. The woman inside continued to chant and sway to the music only she could hear.

The fingers of his right hand curled more tightly around the butt of the 9mm as he braced for a fight. He opened the door with his left hand and stepped inside.

Still humming, the woman turned. "I need you to go to the supply room and get—"

The cigarette dropped from her mouth. She grabbed for her weapon as he shoved her dead friend toward her, causing her to stumble back a step even as she pulled off a shot that went way wide of his position.

A muffled crack was the only noise his sound-suppressed 9mm made as he pumped one shot into her forehead. The woman's finger failed to depress her own trigger a second time. For one extended beat she stood there staring at him before the weapon slipped from her hand and her sizeable bulk followed it to the floor.

Activity stirred beyond the only remaining closed door.

He crossed the room in three strides and flattened against the wall next to the couch.

The door swung inward and a man shuffled out. Forty, forty-five. A hairy beer gut hung over his boxers. A .38 was secured in his right hand.

"What the hell's going on out here?"

Before the startled man could recover from seeing his cohorts dead on the floor, he found himself pinned to the door frame and his right arm wrenched over his head. After a few violent slams against the wall, the .38 clattered to the floor.

The 9mm jammed beneath the scumbag's sagging jowls kept him paralyzed. "Where's the girl?"

The guy blinked as if he'd just awakened from a deep sleep. The craggy lines of his face, the redness of his eyes and the advanced decay of his teeth signaled that his slumber had been anything but natural.

"I dunno what the hell you're talking about."

"The little girl." He jabbed the muzzle deeper into the scumbag's filthy flesh. "Where is she?"

Realization appeared to dawn in the bastard's

expression. "I know who you are. I watch the news." An evil light went on in his eyes as he started to laugh. "Why don't you kill me, tough guy?"

"Where…is…she?" With each word he wedged the weapon deeper into the fatty tissue of that sagging jowl.

"Go ahead," the bastard dared, a sadistic grin stretched across his lips, "pull that trigger. Save the courts a lot of time and trouble—*if* you're man enough."

The finger set against the trigger itched to do just that. The rage overpowered him briefly; the need to erase this mistake of nature from the planet made him shudder with its intensity.

The scumbag laughed louder. "I knew you wouldn't. You don't kill nobody unless they try to kill you first. I can just walk out of here and you won't do a damned thing."

Leaning closer, close enough that there would be no mistaking his words, he warned, "Don't believe for a second that you're going to get off that easy. I want you to rot in a six-by-nine cell for the rest of your stinking life. That's the only reason you're going to live. Now *where is she?*"

Too arrogant or too stupid to feel any fear, the scumbag bit out, "She's in the next room."

One shove sent him to the floor.

The idiot scrambled for the .38.

Two bullets to the brain stopped him cold.

He stepped over the sprawled trash and entered the other room. A stained mattress lay on the floor. No other furnishings. Only the discarded jeans and shirt the scumbag now decomposing in the other room had worn. Images of what had most likely taken place in this room made his guts knot in disgust.

He couldn't think about it, had to find the girl.

His tension shifted to the next level, sent his heart smashing against his sternum as his gaze settled on the door on the other side of the room.

She was here.

He knew it.

The knob rattled as he clasped it with his left hand and turned. The hinges creaked with age as the door swung open.

Total darkness engulfed the room or closet that lay beyond. He reached for the flashlight on his utility belt, switched it on and pointed the beam of light into the room. His heart had started to pound in spite of his efforts to remain calm. This room was about the same size as the adjoining room but pungent with chemical odor. The one window had been boarded up.

Containers filled with necessities of the business being conducted here were stacked against a far wall. Drain cleaner, uniodized salt, coffee filters and anhydrous ammonia, a highly illegal and strictly regulated ingredient. This was the supply room. The idiots had their dangerous ingredients stored in the house with them. Too bad the stupid bastards hadn't blown themselves to hell long ago.

Where was the girl?

His heart rate continued to rise traitorously.

He wasn't wrong. She would be here. Left amid all this poison.

A faint whimper tugged his senses to the opposite corner of the room, where what appeared to be discarded boxes were piled high. He eased in that direction, not quite ready to put his weapon away. Not quite certain of the sound he'd heard.

He moved first one box and then the other. Some contained evidence of more of the accoutrements essential in this illegal operation. Others were empty, their former contents anyone's guess.

Halfway through the mound he saw her.

Curled into a fragile ball of arms and legs and pressed as far into the corner as the rough wood walls would allow. She peered up at him, her eyes wide with fear.

"Don't be afraid," he assured as he pushed the

last of the boxes aside and crouched down in front of her. "No one can hurt you now." Anguish chewed at his insides. Damn these bastards.

He scooped her trembling body into his arms and strode out of that hellhole of a shack, his anger building all over again.

This had to stop.

He had to do all he could, but he feared it would never be enough.

She started to cry, her sobs racking her small body.

"Don't cry, Jesse," he whispered. "You don't have to be afraid anymore. They can't hurt you now."

Chapter Two

Chicago
The Colby Agency
Wednesday 2:10 p.m.

Seated at the small conference table in Victoria Colby-Camp's office, Ann Linker Martin's full attention remained glued to the monitor on the credenza as a previously recorded newscast played. The reporter's grim tone sent shivers spilling across Ann's flesh even before the words penetrated her brain.

"According to Front Royal's chief of police, little Jesse Duncan insists a man wearing a baseball cap took her from the house where she'd been held, then dropped her off at her own front door. As of this hour, the location where Jesse was held is still unknown. No official confirmation has

been given, but residents of Front Royal are convinced that Jesse Duncan was rescued by the East Coast's own Guardian Angel."

Victoria pressed Off on the remote. "I'm sure this isn't the first you've heard of this so-called Guardian Angel."

"I'm very familiar with the story," Ann confirmed. She'd grown up in the Baltimore area, had worked as a consultant to Baltimore's FBI field office. Anything that went on in that territory was of specific interest to her. Six "Guardian Angel" rescues over the past two years had taken place in her hometown. "Considering the airtime this guy is getting," she added, "it would be hard not to have heard of him."

As happy as she was to hear that little Jesse Duncan had been rescued, promoting this man's agenda was just wrong. Whoever he was, he was no Guardian Angel. Since when did angels wear baseball caps? And leave murder victims behind? He was a vigilante, pure and simple.

Guardian Angel was an unidentified suspect who had reportedly rescued around a dozen children in the past four years. Possibly more, possibly going back as far as ten years. The reports were scattered and inconsistent. But they all had one thing in common: the perpetrators of the crimes against the children were, more often than not, discovered dead in one manner or another.

The guy was probably nothing more than an urban legend, a story that picked up momentum after being aired by the media repeatedly. These so-called rescues could be the work of several people or even the original perpetrators of the crimes who'd had a change of heart, prompted by fear, and who hoped to avoid being caught. The one thread of consistency—the baseball cap he supposedly wore—could be an element the police unwittingly introduced to recently rescued victims. The whole world wanted to believe in a Guardian Angel...especially when it came to missing children.

But Ann, the weight of tension crushing down on her shoulders, knew from personal experience that no such creature existed. There were no Guardian Angels. Far too often it was luck of the draw whether a child was recovered after abduction. Without enough evidence, luck was all law enforcement had. Too many times that luck was bad. The odds of finding missing children grew slimmer with every passing hour after the abduction. A great many variables played a part in whether a child was recovered safely or not, but none of them included a Guardian Angel.

Despite this so-called hero's intended good deeds, the man—if he even existed—was nothing more than a murderer himself, in her opinion. He'd get caught one of these days. Or he'd get dead when he encountered a more intelligent criminal. Justice should be left up to those carrying the official credentials.

"You don't see this man as a hero," Victoria suggested candidly.

Ann had her own reasons for finding that line of reasoning exasperating. But she wasn't going there. The past was the past—far better left exactly there. "You want my honest opinion?" she asked just as candidly. When Victoria nodded, Ann admitted, "Based on what I've seen in the media, he's just another killer, not a hero."

Victoria glanced at the blackened monitor. "I'm certain the parents of those rescued children feel differently."

Ann wouldn't argue that point. She was immensely grateful that the children in each of these instances had been saved. But what kind of message were the man's actions sending to the public? And what about all the other children? How did their parents feel? Why were some children rescued by this so-called angel and others not?

The only way to maintain civil order was to

have laws. Vigilante justice was not the answer. Prevention was the key. More stringent laws, stronger punishments.

The apprehension started to tighten uncomfortably around her chest. She wasn't in law enforcement, hadn't really ever been. A consultant, as she'd learned the hard way, didn't count. The sooner she stopped allowing her past to influence her decisions, the sooner she would get on with her future. She had to stop obsessing on things that didn't matter anymore, had to focus on the reason she had been called to Victoria's office this morning. It usually meant she was about to be assigned a new case.

Victoria rose and crossed to her desk. She retrieved a file folder, then returned to her seat at the small conference table. "Katherine Fowler and her family," Victoria began as she opened the file, "live in an intimate upper-class community called Edgewater, an hour's drive outside Baltimore."

Ann wasn't familiar with that particular neighborhood, but she knew the general vicinity. Very upscale.

"Four days ago," Victoria continued, "her only child, Caroline, was abducted from the yard where she was playing not a dozen meters from her mother." Victoria placed a photograph of a little girl on the table in front of Ann. "The FBI and the Arundel County deputies are working around the clock to solve the case. Unfortunately," Victoria said as she placed a report next to the photo, "Caroline appears to be the sixth child in a string of abductions aptly dubbed the Fear Factor case. So far not a single child has been recovered."

Definitely not good. Ann had read numerous articles on Fear Factor. The perpetrators watched for the perfect opportunity, preying on the mother for the ransom in each case.

"Did they use the bank scam for the money transaction?" It amazed her that these guys continued to get away with the same exact ploy. Were the local banks watching for this sort of transaction? Had they briefed their personnel as to what to look for in a stressed customer? Ann didn't see how such a simple maneuver could continue unchecked. Obviously it had.

"According to the chief of police, it's the same MO, down to the mother being left to wait for a call that never comes," Victoria said, her own disbelief evident.

Ann studied the picture of the blond-haired child. No doubt this little girl's mother had seen the news and on some level had recognized her daughter was a victim of the same perps as the other abductions in this case. But how did a mother risk her child's life and go against the pattern? Say no to the kidnappers and go straight to the police?

She didn't. And that was the one unwavering instinct the perps were banking on, no pun intended.

The worst part about this series of kidnappings was that so far the children hadn't been recovered, period. No bodies. No nothing. Only an empty promise to deliver. One theory mentioned by the Bureau's press representative was that the bad guys took the ransom and then sold the children for even more money. Why give up a negotiable asset? Why waste it? The prevailing thinking was that the perpetrators were not pedophiles. To the contrary, they appeared to be savvy businessmen. With an intimate knowledge of how the banking system worked and a burning desire to cash in on the world's leading black-market trade—human trafficking. A shudder started deep down inside her, but Ann bullied it back into submission. Not going there.

"There've been no evidentiary discoveries to date?" Ann asked as she glanced over the report prepared by Arundel County.

"Not a single shred," Victoria confirmed. "Nor

is there anything that ties the different victims or their families together other than tax bracket." Victoria's gaze settled heavily onto hers then. "This is your specialty, Ann. You've worked with the Baltimore Bureau office. You're the perfect choice for this assignment. Katherine Fowler wants her daughter back and she's scared to death that the usual channels are not going to get the job done."

For several seconds after Victoria stopped talking, Ann sat there unable to make an appropriate response.

Yes, she possessed the electronic-banking expertise and the experience with the Baltimore authorities. Those were the very skills that had gotten her noticed by the Bureau. The same Bureau that had ignored her warnings on that final case and caused the death of a child. Ann had sworn that she would never feel that helpless again. That was why she was here working in the private sector, away from all the bureaucratic crap. Working with the Colby Agency had helped her regain her self-confidence, her sense of purpose. It had made her feel capable of going out on that emotional limb of trusting her instincts once more.

Until now…maybe.

"You have a problem with taking this case, Ann?"

"No." Ann laid the report aside and ordered a smile into place to cover the lie. "Absolutely not." Even as she said the words, her stomach clenched.

"This is the highest-profile abduction yet," Victoria noted with a pointed glance at the photo of Caroline Fowler. "That says one significant thing to me—"

"They're getting braver," Ann finished for her, resisting the urge to shift restlessly in her chair. Damn her inability to stop this infernal response. This was a case. Just a case. It wasn't about her or her past.

"None of the law enforcement personnel already involved is going to be happy about your presence," Victoria offered. "You'll be treading into *their* territory, stepping on *their* toes."

"I understand." Ann folded her hands on the table in front of her. She particularly understood that she'd made a few enemies at the Bureau when she'd walked away. "What exactly does Mrs. Fowler want me to do that she believes the Bureau can't?"

Victoria was a very elegant woman. Her dark, all-seeing eyes and coal-black hair streaked silver spoke of wisdom and years on this earth. She had built this agency with her own sweat and tears and a great deal more heartache than she would likely care to confess. But she never asked one of her investigators to do anything she wasn't prepared to do herself. And yet somehow today she looked uncertain of the assignment she was about to give.

She couldn't possibly know Ann's secret. No one did.

"Six children have been wrenched away from their homes and not a single piece of evidence has been found. Katherine Fowler has every right to be concerned that her child will not be found. So—" Victoria exhaled a deep, worrisome sigh "—Mrs. Fowler has retained our agency to find the one man she is certain can rescue her daughter."

Ann knew even before Victoria could say the words. "How am I supposed to do that?" This was a desperate mother grappling at straws. What she was asking would take days or weeks or longer—if it was even possible to lure this so-called Guardian Angel out of seclusion. Little Caroline Fowler probably didn't have hours, much less days or weeks.

"I'm certain you'll find a way," Victoria insisted.

All Ann could do was give it her best shot. Even as the thought formed in her mind, she realized a dozen reasons she would fail before she even started. Her thoughts wandered to the guy with the baseball cap who rescued children from the worst possible situations. Not the guardian-angel persona the press had created but the man himself. No matter how you looked at it, the guy was still a murderer. She'd seen the sketches of him. The baseball cap and the ponytail of long hair were about all any of the kids ever remembered.

How did he choose the missing kids he intended to rescue? Was it about the ones he could find or did he have some sort of method or inside track even the police didn't have?

The better question was, how the hell did she find him? What if it wasn't one guy? Resolving that question could take weeks. Determination fired inside her. She would have to operate under the assumption this was indeed a lone perpetrator. If so, he definitely wasn't a ghost or a phantom. He existed. Ate and slept like everyone else. Someone somewhere knew something. She didn't believe in angels or spiritual guardians of any sort. Criminal or heroic, people were the ones who made things happen. And people made mistakes.

All she had to do was look for his mistakes.

Or maybe she'd just issue him an invitation.

Chapter Three

Fowler home
Edgewater
Thursday 12:05 p.m.

Katherine Fowler was devastated. Her physician had prescribed a heavy-duty sedative, but she refused to take it. The distraught woman considered her daughter's abduction to be entirely her fault, and no one was going to convince her otherwise.

"If she's…dead," Katherine murmured, "I don't think I'll…" Her feeble voice trailed off.

"Mrs. Fowler." Ann took a deep breath in an effort to subdue the adrenaline throttling through her veins. With genuine understanding in her eyes and compassion in her tone, she attempted to relay whatever assurances she could. "I'm sure the

Bureau has told you that there is every reason to operate under the assumption that your daughter is still alive. Until there is evidence indicating otherwise, that won't change. It's important that you hang on to that."

Special Agent Frank Lewis was on the back patio, speaking to the father. There had been a time when Ann had worked closely with Lewis. They'd been friends. Still were, she supposed. That old connection had gotten her past the father, who wanted nothing to do with what he called his wife's ridiculous scheme.

The father, Trey Fowler, a member of a special Homeland Security council, had been out of the country at the time of the abduction. He knew nothing, but there was always the remote chance that his daughter's abduction had something to do with his work. That possibility couldn't be ruled out at this stage in the investigation no matter how much the MO of this case resembled that of another. Lewis had been kind enough to bring Ann up to speed on the way from the airport. But she understood that he'd told her what the Bureau wanted her to know.

Katherine Fowler shook her head. "There's nothing else they can do. They won't be able to find her." A fresh wave of tears spilled down her cheeks. "They haven't found even one of the other five." She scrubbed at her cheeks with the backs of her hands. "That's why we have to find *him*. He's our only hope."

Ann recognized and understood the feeling of being completely alone and helpless. She wished there was something she could do to assuage that horror. But there wasn't. All she could do was attempt to distract her for a little while. "Before we move into that phase of my investigation," she began, "I need you to understand a few vital facts."

Katherine Fowler nodded eagerly. "Whatever I have to do. Anything." She grabbed a wad of tissues and swiped at her nose.

Ann moistened her lips and went for broke. "First of all, you need to be fully aware that the perpetrators in this case watched your family for days or weeks. Every move you made was under a microscope. Intense planning and strategizing went into the decision as well as the move to take your little girl. I'm certain the Bureau emphasized that these people would have found the right opportunity one way or another, it was only a matter of time once the decision to take your daughter was made. Nothing anyone could have done would have stopped them."

Katherine's worried gaze clouded with confusion, and her head moved slowly from side to side. "No. I wasn't watching her closely enough. Then I let them fool me into not calling the police. This *is* my fault."

Ann ordered her heart rate to slow when it stubbornly continued to increase. The annoying constriction around her chest wouldn't abate. She could not let the tension and panic gain so much ground so quickly. She hadn't allowed that to happen in years; she wasn't about to start now. Where was her objectivity? *Focus,* she ordered. *Focus and stay that way.*

"You had no reason to believe your daughter wasn't perfectly safe in your backyard." Ann tried again to reach past the blame Katherine Fowler had heaped onto her own shoulders. "The people who took your daughter are professionals. You have to understand that before we can move forward. This is an essential step, Katherine." She used her first name for emphasis. "I need you to stop fixating on what you should have done and focus on what we can do."

The neighborhood where the Fowler family resided was premiere. There was no reason at all to suspect trouble. The family's feelings of security had been bought and paid for with top dollar. But no amount of money could erase the idea that if she had watched more closely, been more careful, her daughter would not be missing. Still, Ann had to try.

The confusion cleared from Katherine's eyes and she looked directly into Ann's. "I want you to do a press conference for me. Plead with *him* to help my daughter." She shuddered visibly. "My husband won't let me do it. And, quite honestly, I'm in no shape to get in front of a camera." Hope glittered in her eyes for the first time. "But you can do it."

Ann definitely hadn't seen that one coming. "Do you realize how that will expose you and your family to every freak in the state? Maybe even the country?" This was not a sound idea.

"Couldn't we have one of those hotlines?" Katherine straightened her back and lifted her chin ever so slightly in defiance of the paralyzing emotions glittering in her eyes. "There has to be a way to make this happen, and going to the media is the most efficient method I can think of."

Ann wouldn't argue that. She'd already considered that issuing a personal invitation would be the quickest route to getting this guy's attention. The debate revolved around whether or not this so-called Guardian Angel would respond to the invitation. An attempt to summon him in this manner didn't feel right. There were other means—the classifieds, online chat rooms.

"This is what I want," Katherine urged. "Please say you'll help me. There is no one else."

Ann glanced at the French doors and the man pacing restlessly on the other side. Tragedy was already tearing this family apart. As much as Ann wanted to help, this was so not a good idea. But if summoning this man the world called the Guardian Angel was the point, she damn sure couldn't immediately call to mind a more time-efficient way of reaching out to him. "Let me take some time to think about it," Ann offered. "I'll discuss the option with Agent Lewis."

"And he'll shoot it down," Katherine rebutted. "I want this done. Today. Before it's too late." Tears welled in her eyes all over again. "Don't let me down, Ms. Martin. Please."

"I'll do everything possible to get your daughter back," Ann assured her as she stood. "I'll be at the Hilton. You have my cell number."

"You could make the six-o'clock news," Katherine pressed as she pushed unsteadily to her feet. "We could have a response by morning."

"I'll call you at five," Ann promised. "We'll either be doing a press conference at six or I'll have another option on the table for your consideration."

That was the best she could do. She offered her hand, but Katherine ignored it. Instead she grabbed her and hugged her hard. "Please," Katherine whispered. "You're my only hope."

The return drive to the city left Ann feeling damned helpless. As if she'd left something back at the Fowler home. Maybe a little piece of herself. She'd thought she had put these extreme anxiety reactions behind her a long time ago. But today had proven that she still had a good deal of work to do before the past was really behind her. Hell, maybe it never would be.

Agent Lewis wasn't sure his SAC—special agent in charge—was going to be happy about the press-conference proposal. Except for the part about where they might lure the Guardian Angel into a trap. Apparently the Bureau wanted him almost as much as they wanted the people responsible for the Fear Factor abductions. Ann supposed that wasn't so surprising considering a number of people were dead by his hand.

"What's your take on the father?" She and Lewis hadn't really talked about the father yet. The mother was the primary person of interest in the case at this point. But right now Ann needed to know just how much trouble this guy was going to give her. The man was really put out by the involvement of the Colby Agency—Ann in particular. In his opinion, her presence undermined the Bureau's ability to get the job done.

Lewis considered her question a moment as he took the exit to Aris T. Allen Boulevard. "The man is definitely in a position to generate some unpleasant moments for you. He claims he knows of no one who would want to hurt his family like this. But, hey, you don't get that high up the food chain without making some powerful enemies. We're following that avenue as enthusiastically as any other."

She doubted the latter, but that wasn't her problem. Leaning her head back, she tried to relax. Speaking frankly with Lewis wasn't a hardship. She had trusted him when she consulted for the Bureau. She trusted him now. "I'm not sure how I feel about this press conference." It was not going to go over well with local law enforcement and certainly not with the Bureau.

Lewis shrugged. She took his brief pause as an excuse to study his chiseled profile. They had attempted the dating thing a few times, but work always got in the way. The story of her life.

"I think it could be an excellent strategy."

That surprised her. "Really? I doubt your superiors will feel the same way." That was an understatement if she'd ever made one.

Another of those careless shrugs lifted his navy-clad shoulder. He wore the nicer suits, the ones that couldn't be bought right off the rack.

"A press conference might very well draw the Guardian Angel out of seclusion," he submitted. "He might just decide to help. And there's always the chance an announcement like this could scare the unknown subjects who took the girl. If they feel threatened, they might decide Caroline Fowler is too much of a liability to proceed. Anything's possible, Ann." He shot her a sidelong glance. "If you tell anyone I said this, I'll deny it. We're pretty damned desperate at this point."

Ann's tension eased fractionally at his forthrightness and because he didn't take an immediate stand against the notion of a press conference. Maybe the press conference wasn't such a bad idea. She could handle it. All she had to do was take this one step at a time and keep that damned looming panic at bay.

Lewis's cell buzzed.

Ann didn't have to hear the other side of the conversation to know it wasn't an enjoyable one. The term *dressing-down* came instantly to mind. With a firm "yes, sir," Lewis ended the call.

"Let me guess," Ann offered. "They've heard I'm in town and someone isn't happy."

He flashed her a smile that was far more patient than it was amused. “Bingo.”

As Victoria had said, this wasn’t going to be easy by any stretch of the imagination. The Bureau wouldn’t want her involved in any aspect of their investigation. Certainly not in the public eye amidst all the negativity related to law enforcement’s failure to solve a single one of the Fear Factor cases. Not to mention that the Bureau would remember well the last case with which she’d been involved—not one of the associated memories would be pleasant.

“We have a command performance,” Lewis informed her, “with the director.”

Well, well, it sure hadn’t taken Katherine Fowler’s husband long to get the ball rolling. When he’d said he didn’t like this, he’d really meant it.

Chapter Four

Annapolis, Maryland
5:20 p.m.

Kevin Addison was the best public relations agent on the East Coast. But even he, as he had repeated three times in the past half hour, couldn't perform outright miracles. He needed a face to go with the name quickly becoming a megabuzzword in the electronics world.

Tough luck. That wasn't happening.

Addison heaved a breath of frustration and settled his gaze on Nathan's. Nathan Tyler sat behind his big desk, looking exactly like a character from a pirate movie—again, this was according to Addison himself. He loved throwing phrases like that around. Nathan was weary of his attention to this detail.

Addison didn't get it. This was who Nathan was. Addison would be better served if he would simply get used to it. Nathan wasn't changing. He wore his shoulder-length dark hair gathered at the back of his neck. His unyielding jaw (as Addison would put it) was shadowed by a day's beard growth. Nathan dressed as he always did: well-worn jeans and white button-down shirt. All he needed was the eye patch and he would look exactly like a ruthless pirate—again, according to Addison. Every bit as crafty, as well, some would say. And that was exactly the way he liked it. This persona kept the world at bay…which was the point.

"Think, man," Addison railed. "Those dark, almost forbidding good looks could prove an immense marketing tool. Women love that stuff. A big, strong warrior to keep them safe. Hell, some guys like it, too. We should capitalize on those assets. You're the top security software creator on the planet. Everybody wants you. That you look as enigmatic as the concept of what you do only makes you more marketable."

Nathan didn't allow so much as a flicker of acknowledgment in his eyes. He sat there, surrounded by his books. This was what he did when he wasn't flanked by a dozen computer monitors: research.

All sorts—people, places, things, activities—and all a waste of time, in his agent's opinion.

Addison shook his head at his client's continued silence. "You're not listening to me." He rested his hands at the waist of his designer trousers. "It's almost freaky, Nathan. You don't have the first hobby other than these damned books and not a single friend, discounting the few employees allowed access to this—" he gestured magnanimously "—fortress. You need to get out. Take advantage of all your wealth affords you."

Nathan almost laughed at that. If Addison only knew. He had a hobby, all right. One that kept him very busy but that was his secret.

"You can't hide from the limelight forever," his agent went on. "The name Nathan Tyler is synonymous with impenetrability. Nothing gets past your systems. Your company just bagged a multimillion-dollar government contract. They're going to want to see your face, man."

"No."

Addison threw his hands up. "That's perfect. One word. A single gruff syllable." He pointed an accusing finger at Nathan. "I know you can command a better conversation than this. You don't do all your talking with computer keys."

"The answer is still no," Nathan reiterated,

using multiple words and syllables in an effort to convince the man. Or not.

Addison let his chin drop to his chest and swore softly. "Nathan…" He leveled his gaze on his client's once more. "You have a lame-duck CEO running your company. You have me seeing after your best interests in the media. You have a butler, for Pete's sake, who does your shopping. Give me a break here. The whole world wants to know the answer to one question—who is Nathan Tyler?"

"Go away, Addison. I won't change my mind."

If Addison were an easily intimidated man, Nathan would have had him running for his life with just that laser-beam stare. Addison had told Nathan many times that his icy blue eyes could cut through steel. But Addison was in PR. Sticking his head into the lion's mouth was a survival skill. He wouldn't be where he was today if he let the occasional lead-filled gaze or overbearing tone get the better of him. He was determined.

"One of these days, Nathan," he said, his tone somber now, "someone is going to out you. Why let the enemy choose the time and place when you can take control and do that yourself? Right now."

"Is that a threat, Addison?"

Nathan knew from the widening of his long-time friend's eyes that fear had just trickled down his spine like a bead of sweat. That might just be a first. Maybe the boisterous PR agent *could* be intimidated. Nathan used that lethal air he'd been accused of having the same way he used his appearance—as a means of keeping the select few around him at arm's length. Made them all wonder if he was friend or foe. Made them afraid to turn their backs—all except Addison, of course. Nathan usually had to settle for exasperating him.

Some sacrifices were necessary for keeping secrets…for survival.

"No. No," Addison hastened to explain. "You misunderstand my meaning. I'm only saying that nothing stays secret forever. Why not give ourselves the advantage?"

"This conversation is over."

Addison stood. He knew when he'd gone as far as he could. "All right. I'll be in touch with you next week to review those press releases."

Nathan saw no reason to respond to that comment. Idle chatter was not his style.

Addison picked up his briefcase. "Very well. Good evening."

Addison saw himself out of the seventeenth-century mansion. Dead bolts slid into place behind him. Nathan had designed his own home-security system. Addison insisted that Nathan could make himself a new fortune if he decided to venture into that arena. But Nathan Tyler wasn't interested. He had all he needed right here in Annapolis's historic riverfront district. The harbor view was incredible. Despite being nearly four hundred years old, the house was wired with cutting-edge technology and furnished comfortably.

To Addison and the outside world, Nathan appeared to have it all. The only thing missing was the desire to appreciate those assets fully. Addison insisted that Nathan was wasting away behind these ancient walls. Then, each time he dared make such a comment, evidently fearful that he had crossed some unseen line, he would suggest that perhaps he did not understand the creative mind that was both a frightening and fascinating thing.

As long as this relationship continued to make a rich man out of Addison, what the hell was he complaining about?

Nathan picked up the remote on his desk and unmuted the fifteen-inch plasma sitting on the corner of his desk. As usual, the local news channel had overreported what he'd done.

The child was the important element in this story.

Why didn't they focus on the child? On stopping the predators? Outrage whipped through him, setting his teeth on edge.

They would never learn.

It was when they weren't looking, weren't paying attention, that these travesties occurred.

What would it take to wake them up?

He was only one man.

He couldn't save them all.

He closed his eyes and fought back the images. The horrors that still haunted him even after so many years.

No matter how many children he rescued, he couldn't make the images go away.

The one he hadn't saved tortured him the most. Lived inside him, a constant agonizing reminder.

He'd failed.

Even once was too often.

No drug, nothing, would relieve the pain. And he knew. He'd tried them all. He stared at the glass of bourbon waiting patiently on his desk. It didn't actually relieve the pain, but it made him indifferent to its continued existence for a time. Oh, yes, he'd sampled every imaginable distraction. Nothing had ever given him real peace. Not even for a fleeting instant. Still, he emptied the glass, promptly refilled it, then repeated the process.

That was his cross to bear, as they say. He would just have to deal with it.

Nothing could get in the way of what he had to do. And maybe then, when he'd made the ultimate sacrifice, he would find some margin of peace.

The ongoing press coverage on the screen tugged at his attention once more. Special Agent Carson Bailey stepped up to the podium next. He recognized the man as head of Baltimore field operations. He'd seen him in the spotlight before.

Now this might actually be interesting. The Bureau was usually far less easily impressed with rumors and myths. He was sick to death of hearing the reporters wax on about heroes and saviors and shadows in the night.

He was neither. He was just a man with a mission.

Bailey provided an update on the Fear Factor case, which proved nothing more than a rehash of what the public already knew. Zilch. He reassured those within his jurisdiction that the Bureau would do all within its power to protect their children.

Nothing Nathan hadn't heard before.

He almost changed the channel, but then a new face captured his attention.

The young woman was introduced as Ann Martin, no federal or local law enforcement rank included. He hadn't seen her before. Luxurious long blond hair. Distracting green eyes. She stepped up to the microphone, looking a little nervous, and launched into a lengthy discussion of how important it was to generate community support during a time such as this. Even with her voice shaking ever so slightly, her words carried far more meaning than the words of those who had spoken before her. As she plowed onward with her statement to the press, the scope of her assertions went beyond the Duncan case, beyond the missing children in the Fear Factor case. She spoke with conviction, with fierce determination on how the parents of those children suffered.

His instincts roused further, pushing aside the warm alcohol haze he'd accomplished with the bourbon.

It wasn't so much the words she said that held his attention. It was the explosive passion with which she spoke. As if she understood the horrendous fear the parents suffered. As if she could feel the pain of the children.

As if...she had personal experience.

He leaned forward...reached out and touched the screen as she hammered away at her audience—an audience of more than just the folks she wanted to reassure. She was speaking to those who committed crimes against children. She was speaking to *him*.

A surge of excitement flowed through his veins.

He traced the outline of her face, felt a knowing smile twist his lips.

"You know, don't you?"

And then she did the last thing he expected. She asked for his help. Rattled off a number he should call anytime, day or night.

"Ann Martin." He inclined his head and studied her face as she thanked the audience and the press. "What are you up to?"

Chapter Five

Baltimore City Hall
6:40 p.m.

The press had finally started to filter out of the lobby. Dozens of agents and police officers lingered, discussing the case, talking about the good old days. This one had been an all-employees press conference—Bureau personnel as well as every uniform available. The powers that be had wanted a show of force. They'd gotten their wish.

Ann tried to act interested in the discussion she'd been dragged into by a former colleague, but one thought kept pounding in her brain: she had to get out of here. Now.

The overwhelming sense of doom had started to press in around her a mere sixty seconds after she'd walked away from the podium, following furiously on the heels of the raging adrenaline that had taken complete control of her brain the second she opened her mouth in front of the cameras. She should never have let herself get so worked up. When she'd started to launch her statement, simple and to the point, something had gone wrong. She'd gone off on a damned tangent, and years of buried history had spewed forth as if she'd lost total influence over her tongue.

Dread congealed in her gut. God, she'd lost it completely. On camera, at that. The whole city—the nation—had been watching. It would be a miracle if she was allowed anywhere near the people involved in this case once the postmortem of the press conference had been conducted. The Bureau would be outraged and Victoria Colby-Camp would be utterly confused. Where was the cool, controlled investigator she had hired? That would be merely one of many questions Victoria would ask herself.

"Good job, Martin." Bailey patted her arm. "I liked the passion you put behind your plea. I'm certain there wasn't anyone watching who didn't feel it."

She managed a rigid smile in spite of the shock his words evoked. "Thank you, sir."

"Publicly appealing to the Guardian Angel was

a stroke of genius," Bailey added. "We need that vigilante off the streets."

Somehow Ann managed to hold that stiff expression in place while he congratulated her once more. When SAC Bailey had moved on to interface with far more distinguished guests, she sucked in a shaky breath. Maybe she hadn't blown it completely. Maybe she hadn't gone off track as badly as she'd thought. Time would certainly tell.

Lewis appeared next to her. He grinned. "You had the crowd mesmerized."

"Thanks." That dread she'd felt thickening in her stomach started to churn in spite of the compliments. Her palms had begun to sweat. She needed to get out of here before the symptoms became visible. "You know..." She struggled to keep her voice even as she spoke. "I think I'll call it a day." She looked around for the best escape route. She wanted out of here without running into anyone from the press...or anyone else, for that matter. She hadn't even checked in to her hotel yet.

As if reading her mind, Lewis angled his head to the right. "They keep the west corridor closed off during these things. Go that way and you won't have to worry about being chased by the press."

She nodded jerkily. "Good idea."

Thank God Lewis headed off another agent who called her name. Ann walked as fast as she could without breaking into a dead run. She gulped in another deep breath, tried to hold it as long as possible before releasing. Deep breath, hold, release. It was supposed to work. Wasn't doing any good this time, though.

As Lewis had said, the west corridor was blocked off, but the guard recognized her and allowed her to pass. She saw the exit doors in the distance, but somehow they kept getting farther and farther away.

No matter how fast she walked, she just wasn't getting closer.

Her heart thundered, racing for a finish line only her hysteria recognized. Her skin felt cold and damp. Bile rose into her throat.

Oh, God.

Ladies' room on her right.

She glanced behind her. No one coming. She ducked into the ladies' room and braced her trembling body against the wall.

Slow, deep breaths.

The ragged sounds echoed as if she were suffering from an asthma attack.

Slowly inhale. Count to ten. Slowly exhale.

She closed her eyes and tried to relax. Ordered

herself to stop fighting the terror…to roll with it and let it pass. Her fingers clenched, but she consciously unclenched them. *Relax. Calm down. Deep breaths.*

Her heart thudded so hard she could barely hear for the blood roaring in her ears. Her limbs tingled as if they'd gone to sleep with her standing up.

The pressure on her chest increased, felt like a ton of bricks stacked one by one until she couldn't breathe. Fear wrapped around her every thought, wouldn't let go.

Relax, Ann. Just relax.

She'd been through this before. But it had been years. She reminded herself she wasn't in actual danger. All she had to do was reclaim control, calm down and let this thing go.

Four whole years. She hadn't had a full-blown panic attack in four years.

"Damn it."

That first case she'd consulted on for the Bureau she'd suffered an episode, but she'd caught it in time, had headed it off. No one had been the wiser when it was over. But this…this had sneaked up on her.

Today she'd lost all control.

Today the adrenaline had taken over.

She knew the cause. She'd suffered with panic attacks for a dozen years. But then, her last year of graduate school, they'd abruptly stopped. Granted, she'd worked hard to recognize the aura before the full-blown attack hit, but her life had done a major turnaround and that had been the significant factor in moving past those debilitating episodes.

She'd taken charge of her life.

No way was she going to let the irrational fear take over again. Not now. She'd only just gotten started in her new career. This was right where she wanted to be. She had to regain full authority over her emotions.

Starting this minute.

She pushed away from the wall and took a moment to splash cold water on her face. Her reflection told her just how much power this episode had wielded. Even now the terror lingered in her eyes, attempted to steal the air right out of her lungs.

"You have to be stronger than this. Don't let those old demons back in."

Squaring her shoulders, she looked again, deep into those jade eyes she'd inherited from her father. There was her confidence. It hadn't deserted her. This case had tipped the scales against her, but that wasn't what had started this whole plunge into the past.

It was those damned reports about the Guardian Angel. He had haunted her dreams for weeks now, though she had refused to admit it. She'd tried to block the crazy fixation developing, but she'd lost that battle. On a purely intellectual level she understood her interest in this so-called hero. But on all other levels she resented his intrusion into her life.

He represented the loss of hope and the major disappointment that motivated far too many of the fears she had suffered so long ago; all that he stood for fueled the bitterness she still felt at times even now. None of which was completely rational.

"No living in the past," she told the woman looking back at her. "No obsessing. No fear. *Encounter, learn, overcome.*"

That was her motto. Life wasn't always kind. But she wasn't the only one who'd suffered. Not by a long shot. In fact, she was damned lucky to have survived the worst fate had thrown in her path.

All she had to do was remember her motto. No matter how bad things got as she adjusted to the evolving demands of her new career path. No matter how terrifying the case she was assigned. She could handle anything that came her way.

Encounter, learn, overcome.
It was the only way to defeat the demons.
Past and present.
It was the only way to move on.

Chapter Six

Baltimore Hilton
7:45 p.m.

Ann wasn't in the habit of bringing men back to her hotel room when on assignment, but this was different. Special Agent Frank Lewis was doing her a major favor. She needed all the information he would give her.

"This—" he indicated the stack of file folders he plopped onto the table "—is what I'm allowed to share with you."

Director Bill Waters hadn't been happy at all to learn that the services of the Colby Agency had been retained by Katherine Fowler. He was even less pleased that Ann was the investigator, but there wasn't a hell of a lot he could do about it. Still, making the press conference a joint effort had been his idea. Since he couldn't prevent an American citizen from doing what she would as far as seeking outside help in finding her daughter, he'd decided that if he was in charge, things would be under his control. So he'd ordered SAC Bailey to cooperate—to a degree.

Ann had allowed those in charge to think that control was theirs for the taking. Worked like a charm.

"Walk me through it," she said to Lewis as she peeled off her jacket and tossed it on the bed. She was exhausted. She hadn't gotten much sleep last night and she didn't see that trend changing anytime soon.

"The first victim went missing three weeks ago." Lewis opened the folder on top to display the photo of a six-year-old girl and her relevant statistics. "Three days later a second child was taken." Another folder opened to reveal the pertinent details of the victim.

Ann studied the photo of the dark-haired girl in the second folder. "Then the game shifted gears." She'd seen on the news where a third and then a fourth child had gone missing within mere days of the second abduction, putting the toll to four in just under two weeks.

"Exactly." Lewis opened the other two folders.

"Then two more within the past ten days. Including Caroline Fowler."

Ann studied the faces of the children. "No connections?" Her gaze leveled with his. "Nothing whatsoever?"

"Tax bracket. Geography." He turned his palms upward. "That's it."

Four girls, two boys. Varying ages but all under ten. All from the Baltimore area.

"What about known sex offenders in the area? Pedophiles?" The theories were limitless. "How much follow-up has been conducted there?"

She walked to the minibar and grabbed a bottle of water. She waved the bottle in invitation.

Lewis shook his head in response to her offer of refreshment. "We've had uniforms knocking on every door in the databank, without results."

Like looking for a needle in a haystack. That was the problem with cases like this. Without evidence or a reasonable way to develop a profile, there was little they could do with any realistic expectations of success. A massive brick wall loomed in front of them, and climbing over or going around looked highly unlikely at this time. What they needed was a miracle.

Funny part was, she didn't believe in miracles.

She dropped into one of the chairs flanking the

table. The drapes were drawn on the floor-to-ceiling window overlooking the parking lot. "Tell me about the bank transactions." It was hard to believe that an electronic transfer had stumped the Bureau.

He pulled out the other chair, straddled it and then propped his arms on the back. "That's the simple part. The victim's mother makes the transfer in person. The receiving account is numbered." He laughed, a dry, humorless sound. "Unfortunately, that's where things get complicated. The money is shuffled through more than a dozen accounts, ending up in Switzerland amid millions of other anonymous accounts. The owner of the account is totally untraceable. Hell, the last time we checked, the balance on the account hadn't changed. The money's just sitting there. It's weird."

Ann felt a frown pull at her brow, nudging at a distant headache she'd just as soon not deal with. Seeing the balance, electronically speaking, wasn't a problem. It was gaining access to the profile of the account holder that proved impossible if the holding entity refused to cooperate. Why wouldn't the balance have been manipulated already?

"Maybe it isn't about the money," she commented, a thought spoken.

She spread the photos of the children into a lineup. No similarities in coloring or facial features. Just six missing kids, all with parents who could afford to pay a hefty sum for their return.

Only they hadn't been returned.

"We've considered every imaginable scenario," Lewis assured her. "We're still toying with several possibilities. The problem is, unless a child is returned or a body is discovered—a mistake of some sort—that's all we'll have. It's difficult to formulate a profile with nothing but an MO."

He was right about that. Ann ran her fingers through her hair, willed the brewing ache away. She needed to eat. She needed sleep.

"Why don't I take you out to dinner?" Lewis offered. He pushed out of his chair and turned it back into the table. "You have to be starving. There's a decent restaurant right here in the hotel."

She started to say no, but room service just didn't sound appetizing tonight. Maybe she just didn't want to be alone after her harrowing reaction to the press conference. Somehow she had to get those ancient demons under control. Distraction usually worked.

"Sounds good." She got to her feet and shouldered back into her jacket. As much as she hoped falling into that bed a little later would precede a good night's sleep, there was no guarantee. Food would help her relax and maybe put off this damned headache.

BY THE TIME THE waiter brought the after-dinner coffee Ann was really glad she had decided to join Lewis for dinner. They had tossed more scenarios back and forth and he'd let a few additional details slip…maybe on purpose. In any case, the time spent had proven quite beneficial.

"You know," Lewis said, his tone candid, "that the director only decided to go along with your involvement in the case because he wants Guardian Angel."

Yes, she understood that. "That makes us even," she confessed. "We're both using each other. If we accomplish our missions, then we'll both be satisfied."

A grin hitched up one corner of the agent's mouth. "Touché." Then his face turned serious again. "The Bureau has acknowledged their mistakes in that final case you worked, Ann."

They were not going there. "That subject is off-limits, Lewis." That case was over. There was no going back. The kid died. No amount of apologies or reassessments would bring her back.

He nodded. "I understand. I just needed to be sure you knew that."

Back to the reason she was here. "I'd like to talk about this Guardian Angel a little more. But first—" she rose from her chair and dropped her linen napkin across her seat "—I need to take a private moment."

He stood. "You're sure I can't talk you into that dessert?" The chuckle that followed told her he regretted bringing up the past.

She pressed her hand to her stomach. "No, thanks." With a pointed nod at him, she added, "Order that cheesecake I know you're dying to have and organize your thoughts on this guy. We still have a lot to talk about, you know."

Ann crossed the dining room and followed the narrow hall to the ladies' room. Her heels clicked on the polished marble. As instinctive as breathing, she scanned the row of stalls. Deserted. Letting go a weary sigh, she took a moment to inspect her reflection in the generous mirror hanging over the marble sinks. She looked a fright. Dark circles under her eyes. The makeup she had applied so carefully that morning was nothing more than a negligible film now.

Shoving a handful of hair behind her ear, she entered the nearest stall and closed the door. As she slid the slim latch into place, the lights went out.

Her breath mired in her throat. For five seconds she wasn't sure what had just happened. Then the distinct sound of rubber soles on the marble floor warned that she wasn't alone.

Damn it. She'd left her purse on the counter. Her cell phone and her pepper spray were in there. She hadn't planned to carry a weapon on this assignment. Mere hours into the assignment and she'd already made her first mistake. Damn it!

"Ms. Martin?"

Goose bumps rushed over her skin at the sound of the deep, deep voice whispering her name. Her heart lunged.

"Yes?" It wasn't as though he didn't know who she was. She braced her hands against the door and prepared to prevent an intrusion.

"You requested a meeting."

She knew a moment's panic. The next instant it was replaced by anticipation.

"Yes, I did." She dug way down deep for her courage. "But how am I supposed to know if you're the man I want to see? The hotline has already fielded thousands of calls. At least a hundred claimed to be Guardian Angel."

That he didn't walk away sent her instincts into the danger zone.

"There were three degenerates at the scene where Jesse Duncan was being held. Two men, one woman. All three are dead, one with a snapped neck and two with bullets to the brain."

Well, he had that right. "You could have gotten

that from the press coverage." She was relatively certain the causes of death had not been reported, but she wasn't one hundred percent positive.

"The female wore an MP3 player."

The images of the crime scene photos Lewis had shown her flashed through her mind. Another accurate detail. Another bout of shivers rushed along her limbs.

"And the lowlife with the broken neck was wearing a T-shirt with a rock band logo emblazoned across his chest."

Her body temperate abruptly dropped a degree. "Okay, so you know what the crime scene looked like. I'm afraid that doesn't prove you're who you say you are. You could be a cop or a Fed trying to undermine my participation in this investigation."

Even as she made that last statement, her fingers went to the latch. If this was really him—the Guardian Angel—this was her opportunity to see him face-to-face. No one could ID him. This could be the perfect opportunity to find out exactly who she was dealing with.

Even as her fingers poised to slide the latch free, that intriguing baritone cut through the silence as if he'd reached right inside her head and read her mind. "I don't think you really want to do that just yet."

She froze. "You know what I want?" Ann said, shifting the attention to her statement in the press conference and away from the idea that he'd estimated her next move so easily. That part made her more than a little nervous.

"I know what you want."

The flailing in her chest morphed to a dead-on crash into her sternum. "Can you help me? There's a sizeable reward for the return of the Fowler child."

Five, ten, fifteen seconds passed in thickening silence. Ann opened her mouth to say more, when he spoke.

"I have no interest in the reward."

This guy couldn't be for real.

"That's an incredibly noble statement, sir," she returned before her brain could halt her tongue. "It makes me curious about your motives."

"Did you call me here to satisfy your curiosity or to find six missing children?"

Fury charged through her. "If you know where these children are, why haven't you rescued them already?" Indignation fueled the flames of her anger. That was the problem with this guy. How did he decide who deserved to be rescued? How did he find a particular missing child when the police couldn't?

"I didn't say I knew where they were."

Those angry emotions twisted into frustration. "If you can't help me find Caroline Fowler, then why did you seek me out?" She pressed her hand to the place on the door that corresponded with his eye level, tried to imagine his image on the other side.

"You have no interest in the other five children?"

Now she was just plain old ticked off. "Of course I'm interested in the other children. But Katherine Fowler hired my agency to help bring her child home. My client is my first obligation."

More of that unbearable silence. The need to open the door, to see his face, was nearly overwhelming. But somehow she resisted.

"You'll be hearing from me, Ms. Martin. Tell Katherine Fowler that I will find her child…along with the other five."

"How can you make a promise like that?" The FBI hadn't even been able to form a viable theory, much less a profile on the unsubs. Not a shred of evidence had been discovered at any of the crime scenes. They had nothing.

What kind of power trip was this guy on?

The silence was different this time.

He was gone.

Ann jerked the door open and peered into the darkness.

Nothing.

She rushed to the door. Hit the switch to flood the room with light.

The stalls were empty.

Whoever had been here had vanished.

Just like a ghost…or an *angel.*

Too bad she didn't believe in either one.

Chapter Seven

Friday, 2:03 a.m.

She was afraid.

It was so dark. How would she ever find her way home?

Ann's heart thumped hard in her nine-year-old chest. But she wasn't nine anymore. She was an adult.

A dream. This had to be a dream.

She shook her head, told her eyes to open. But she couldn't wake up.

The bad man might hear her.

She had to run.

Run faster.

The limbs and bushes scratched at her bare legs. Tears were rolling down her cheeks, but she didn't make a sound.

He might hear.

Run. Run and don't look back.

If he found her...

"No!" Ann bolted upright.

It was dark.

Where the hell was she?

The air sawing in and out of her lungs, she forced her mind to focus, her eyes to see.

Where was she?

Another minute was required for her brain to clear.

Hotel. Baltimore.

Her heart rate instantly slowed and her breathing slowly returned to normal. She was okay. Safe.

No reason to be afraid.

Her skin felt clammy with sweat. She threw the sheet back and dropped her feet to the floor. The artificially cooled air made her shiver.

"Just a stupid dream."

She shoved the damp hair back from her face and trudged to the bathroom. After flipping on the light, she braced against the sink and stared at her reflection. The remnants of fear still haunted her eyes.

Damn it.

She hated when she let those damned nightmares invade her sleep. She was supposed to be over that part of her past.

"Yeah, right."

A long, hot shower would relax her tense muscles. She definitely needed a shower. With one firm turn, she started the spray of water and then stripped off the boxers and tee that were her favorite sleeping attire. Once her hair was secured in a clip, she climbed into the steam-filled shower and started the necessary steps toward relaxing.

This was ridiculous. She hadn't had a panic attack in ages. And now this.

"You're going backward, Martin."

She washed her skin, let the liquid heat release the tension in her facial muscles first, then her shoulders and down her spine. The deep rasp of that voice invaded her attempt at shutting out the world.

I know what you want.

Ann's eyes opened.

She had walked out of that ladies' room to an empty corridor. The exit at the end of the corridor had led to the rear parking lot, but there hadn't been anything out there except parked vehicles. Nothing out of the ordinary in the dining room as she had returned to her table. No one out of place. No new arrivals or departures.

She'd chosen not to mention the incident to Lewis.

The voice had not been her imagination. No

way. But there was no way to prove what she had heard, so why bother? The fewer questions, the better.

But that wasn't the real reason she had kept the incident to herself. The Bureau was already skeptical of her involvement; she wasn't about to bring up anything that might make them more so.

Hearing the voice of a man who had abruptly disappeared wasn't exactly going to lend credibility to what she had to offer. The Bureau knew about her long-ago past. It was all right there in her personnel file. They could easily suggest that this particular case had resurrected old demons. Not to mention her relationship with the Bureau, considering that final case they had worked together, was tenuous at best.

She turned off the water and shoved the curtain aside. Maybe she couldn't control 24-7 the possibility of the past intruding, but she could damn sure work around it. Anyone who thought otherwise was mistaken. She would not allow this case to be about what happened three years ago. Or twenty years ago.

This was her case. She would get the answers she needed and rescue Caroline Fowler. End of story.

When she'd dried her body, she smoothed a

little moisturizer on her skin, then ran a brush through her hair. She watched her long blond hair fall back against her shoulder with each stroke. Caroline Fowler had long blond hair. The image of running through the woods as a child, as Ann had in the nightmare, barged into her consciousness, then somehow evolved into a picture of Caroline running through the woods near the Fowler home.

Ann tossed the brush aside and went to her suitcase, which she had not yet unpacked. She dragged out the one pair of jeans she had brought along and a black T-shirt and skullcap. As the idea forming in her head gained momentum, she rushed to drag on her clothes, then tugged on the pair of running shoes she never left home without. Running every day was her one commitment to staying fit. She had no time or patience for gyms or routines. Pounding the pavement usually kept the panic attacks at bay, as well. Truth was, she stuck with the running more for the latter than the former.

Maybe a middle-of-the-night excursion would do her good considering the way she'd lost control today. And doing it at the scene of the crime would allow her mind to free-associate...to connect with the victim. Maybe even with the kidnapper.

Anything to get her out of this hotel.

A LITTLE MORE THAN an hour later, she was parked at the county road next to the long, winding drive that led to the Fowler lakefront home.

Ann pressed the remote to lock the car doors, then shoved the pepper spray into one hip pocket and the keys to the rental in the other. A flashlight in hand, she tucked her ID and cell phone in her front pocket in case she happened upon security. The house and a one-hundred-yard perimeter of the property were considered a crime scene. Her current position was some five hundred yards from the house. Accessing the property from here, she could easily follow the route the kidnappers utilized.

She surveyed the woods on either side of the road. There were few houses along this stretch. Most properties consisted of ten or more acres, ensuring plenty of privacy between the residences. The sprawling county road was interrupted only by the occasional drive on the left or right. No streetlamps to diminish nature. Nothing but the moonlight and unobstructed stars to light the night.

Without the aid of the flashlight just yet, she followed the winding drive to the spot Forensics had indicated as the pickup point for the unknown subjects. A car had waited—Ann paused on the pavement—until whoever had taken the girl had returned. Exactly one hundred yards from the house.

She shined the beam of her flashlight over the woods that marched right up to the lushly landscaped lawn of the backyard. The lake bordered the property in front of the house.

With three hundred feet between the point of abduction and the getaway car, they'd had to be sure of Katherine Fowler's reaction as well as their ability to get in and back out with the kid in an extremely efficient manner.

Taking her time, Ann followed the path Forensics had marked with yellow crime-scene tape wherever a broken limb or smashed clump of underbrush indicated hurried foot traffic had recently covered.

As she traveled that stretch of the woods, Ann focused on imagining the scene. Forensics had determined that only one person, adult, probably male, had approached the house and then left carrying the child. The change in the depth of footprint impressions, the few that had been found, indicated he'd carried the child in his right arm.

If Caroline hadn't screamed or put up a struggle—and Forensics didn't think she had—she'd most likely been drugged. Something fast-acting, like an inhalant.

Ann clicked off the light before approaching

the yard. She stood very still behind the cover of trees and surveyed the well-lit area. The patio was highly visible from her position. Caroline had been playing there. Her mother had worked only a few yards away.

How had the unknown subject in a span of no more than two or three minutes lured a five-year-old from her afternoon tea party with a dozen or so dolls?

Ann turned back to the deep, dark forest behind her. Had Caroline approached these woods in the light of day without an inkling of fear? What bait had the unsub used? Another doll? Another child? Katherine had said her daughter had made frequent visits into the house to get more of her dolls. Had she been taken from inside the house? That part was unclear as of yet.

Forensics had found numerous monitoring devices installed inside the house weeks ago, but none were traceable back to the buyer, much less the installer. The hardware had been run-of-the-mill surveillance toys available online or in any spy gadget store. Every move the family had made had been monitored for two weeks or more.

These guys were good. Ann tried to imagine the kind of people who would go to this much trouble to take a child and then only demand half a million in ransom when, clearly, more had been available.

Because half a million was much easier to move electronically at a moment's notice. Oh, yes, they were good. Very good. They left nothing to chance. Every step had been carefully planned and calculated down to the second, to the most finite details. The transfer was ingenious, she had to confess. The abduction technique flawless.

But there had to be a mistake somewhere. These abductions were planned and executed by humans. As seemingly flawless as they were, there had to be something they were missing between point A and point B. The child was taken, the ransom demand made. Then nothing. No point C—no drop-off, no dead body, no nothing.

Ann snapped her flashlight back on and slowly retraced her path, taking care not to disturb the areas designated as evidentiary. Where had the unsubs taken these children for safekeeping?

The flight trail was as cold as the money trail. Impossible to track.

The vehicle tracks and shoe prints were made by commonly available tires and shoes. Nothing traceable. Totally nondescript.

There was no one to have witnessed anything.

All the abductions had been handled in the same manner: no witnesses left behind and no evidence.

Lewis had promised to let her look at the bank records tomorrow. She really doubted there was anything she could add to what Quantico had already assessed, but she would give it her best shot.

That was the problem with numbered accounts held in places like Switzerland and the Cayman Islands: they were completely anonymous, the countries neutral. Uncovering the identity of the account owner was next to impossible under the best of circumstances.

Ann hesitated. Her senses replayed the last couple of moments. She'd heard a sound she hadn't made. Maybe. She turned off the flashlight and faded into the night.

There it was again.

Reaching for her pepper spray, she started a slow, noiseless one-eighty turn to survey the darkness behind her.

"Don't turn around."

It was *him*.

That deep, deep voice sent a new rush of adrenaline surging through her veins.

Guardian Angel.

Chapter Eight

The woman froze.

"Are you following me?" Ann Martin asked, her voice damned steady for a woman alone in the dark with a stranger.

Nathan considered her stance. Hands in the air. Feet wide apart. She was prepared to fight if the need arose. She'd had nearly identical training as the federal agent cohorts she once worked with, but she wasn't even close to his level. His gaze skimmed her body. The formfitting T-shirt and jeans didn't leave any room for concealing a weapon. There was the can of defense spray in her hip pocket.

His attention settled on the tight knit cap that covered her hair. It was a shame to hide such a lush mane. She certainly didn't look like his idea of a private detective. But looks were often deceiving. He was an expert at creating illusions. Perhaps *she* was an illusion designed to do exactly what she appeared to be accomplishing: drawing him into a trap.

Someone was definitely doing exactly that.

"Yes," he said in answer to her question. He claimed the final step between, positioning himself so close he felt her tremble of uncertainty. Well trained or not, she was still a woman and much smaller than him. "I am following you, Ms. Martin."

Her pause was filled with the silence of the night that enveloped them so completely. No breeze, no scurrying of wildlife…just the weight of the darkness and the thickness of the lingering heat of a September day.

"Why?"

Fair question, but the answer should be more than obvious. "We're both looking for the same thing. The children."

She slowly lowered her hands to her sides. "I was under the impression you worked alone."

Now she was trolling for information. He had known, if given the chance, she would. "Things have changed."

Another of those lengthy hesitations expanded between them.

"Changed how?" she ventured.

"I received a message giving me the location of the first victim in the Fear Factor abductions."

He felt her tension escalate, heard the slight shift in her respiration.

"Kira Robbins?" Disbelief colored her tone.

"Yes." Kira had been the first victim to be snatched from her own backyard. The image of long dark hair and big brown eyes filtered into his thoughts. If Kira was alive, there was hope for the others.

More of that silence that spoke volumes about how much she did not trust him steeped the air.

"This was an e-mail? A phone call?"

Her tone was openly skeptical. Not that he could blame her for feeling so; his own skepticism still nagged at him more than he would prefer.

"I was left a private invitation in an online chat room." Even now it felt surreal. He hadn't been given this information just to make someone's life interesting. There was an agenda and a motivation. "The invitation included the child's name and location as well as what time she could be picked up."

"So this invitation could have been from anyone, including a psycho who's looking for attention."

"That's possible, but I don't think so." He needed her cooperation, though he had no idea how this alliance was going to work out. No idea at all.

"Look." She set her hands on her hips, adopting a stance to match the skepticism that had evolved into an openly dubious attitude. "I don't know who you are or what your game is, but you surely can't expect me to believe that you got a message giving you the location of a victim the FBI can't find."

That was the reaction he'd expected. "Actually, I don't really care what you believe. My only concern is the child. You'll either take the risk and trust me or you won't."

Five, ten, fifteen seconds ticked off. Then she said, "So now you're saying you need me to help you get this done?"

Did she think he wouldn't notice the way her fingers moved ever closer to the self-defense nuisance in her back pocket?

"Whoever sent me this information has an agenda," he explained, his frustration beginning to stir. "An agenda that likely includes outing me or…worse. I may need a distraction. That's where you come in."

"Why didn't you just call the police with this information? Or the FBI?"

He grabbed her hand just as her fingers wrapped around the cylinder. "Because," he said as he held on when she attempted to jerk her hand away, "I'm reasonably sure the Bureau doesn't want to play nice."

Then she did exactly what he had known she would. She twisted to face him. The moonlight provided just enough illumination to showcase her fury.

"What makes you think I'll play nice?"

He kept his fingers locked tightly around her wrist. "Because we're alike, Ms. Martin." A lot more so, he was pretty sure, than she would suspect.

Ann ordered herself to breathe. Stay calm. If this guy wanted to hurt her, he would have done so already. The fingers manacled around her wrist burned her skin. He was taller than she'd expected, six-two or -three maybe. The baseball cap blocked the meager moonlight, ensuring she couldn't make out any real details. Except the mouth. There was a hard set to his mouth…yet the lips were cut surprisingly full.

Focus on the matter at hand. "I don't know what the hell you're talking about," she tossed back. "I don't go around killing people for their crimes. That's why we have a justice system. I doubt we're alike at all."

Those overfull lips slid into a smile. "Think about it for a while and then you'll know."

She jerked her hand away. This time he let go.

"If you have a location, why are we standing around here talking?"

It took every ounce of determination she possessed not to back off. He had invaded her personal space, stood toe-to-toe with her. If there was any chance at all that this guy was for real, she couldn't afford to make a wrong move. She would work with the devil himself if it meant saving those children.

Instead of answering her question, he manacled her hand once more, pivoted and headed in the direction of the main highway.

She commanded herself to go along, not to resist. Whatever his game, she needed to know if there was an inkling of truth in what he said. Even though her services had been retained to find the Fowler child, finding the first child that had gone missing would be a start. If the child was alive, there was always the chance she would remember something that would help the authorities find the rest of the children.

Ann was grasping at straws. The guy dragging her through the woods could be a total nut job.

He'd taken a great deal more care with hiding his vehicle than she had. She'd simply pulled over to the side of the road. Not him. He'd turned into one of the private drives and eased off the pavement far enough to conceal his black SUV from the main road.

Three feet from the passenger-side door she stalled, forcing him to stop.

One hand on the door, he turned back to her. "Changed your mind?"

Her heart thudded against the wall of her chest. Getting into this vehicle with him was, in essence, surrendering to him. As badly as she wanted to learn if this man truly was the Guardian Angel, as much as she wanted to find that child, she had to be reasonable. This man could be a psycho.

"I don't even know your name," she countered. "I'd be a pretty big fool to go anywhere with you." She glanced back toward the main road. "Maybe I should follow in my own car."

"Kira Robbins has in her possession a brown teddy bear wearing a red jumper. She never lets the toy out of her sight. Not even when a stranger grabs her from the homemade wooden swing hanging from the oak tree in her backyard."

Adrenaline rushed through her veins. "Where did you get that information?" Those details had not been released to the media. The Bureau and the local cops involved were the only ones who knew. What if he had taken the children? That would make total sense. He might be watching the cops do their job, would have seen Ann with Agent Lewis. The theory that the Guardian Angel was really the abductor of the missing children and that he used their return as a way to gain glory trickled into her head.

"The same place I got the location where she can be picked up."

He opened the door. The interior light didn't come on.

For a span of time that felt like a mini eternity she stood there unable to climb into the SUV… unable to run like hell. Every instinct screamed at her to run, to use her cell phone to call for help.

But she couldn't take the chance. If he was telling the truth…

She wasn't about to take any risks with a child's life.

Before she could second-guess herself again, Ann climbed into the passenger seat. He rounded the hood and slid behind the wheel.

A dozen reasons why this was surely a mistake bombarded her as he pulled the SUV back out onto the main road. Ann had worked with the Bureau for years. She was usually very good at her job. But tonight she couldn't seem to pull her rational side together. There was only the desperation she felt for the child. The hope that if they found Kira Robbins alive, it was possible to do the same with the others, all the way to Caroline

Fowler. And then there was the possibility of bringing a killer to justice.

She stole a glance at him as she silently repeated the license plate number of the SUV over and over. If she could remember the number, she might be able to track down just who this guy was with a simple phone call.

Shifting her attention from the highway to his profile, she studied the details as best she could with nothing more than the dim glow from the dash to provide illumination. Square jaw. Those unusually full lips and really long hair. He had it pulled back in a ponytail. Dark T-shirt and jeans. The baseball cap was black, as well, and displayed no visible logo.

"You won't find me in any of your databases," he warned.

Who the hell was this guy? That he could read her so easily disturbed her on a whole other level.

"I don't suppose it would do me any good to ask your name? After all, you do know mine." She recognized the futility in expecting him to play by any professional code. If—major if—he was this so-called Guardian Angel, he didn't play by anyone's rules.

"I could tell you, but I'm afraid that would complicate our relationship."

Relationship?

All the uncertainty and that inkling of fear she'd barely kept at bay vanished, replaced by outrage. "You do know that you can't keep getting away with what you're doing, right? I mean, you've killed how many people now? Six, seven? They're going to catch you eventually or your luck is simply going to run out."

He glanced at her, the dim glow from the dash giving her a glimpse of startling blue eyes. "You're probably right." Another look, this one lingering a beat or two longer. "But not tonight."

HE TOOK I-695 TO North Point Road.

Ann recognized the area, North Point State Park. She'd been here a couple of times. Once for a hike with friends, another time on a missing-persons case.

The park covered more than one thousand acres and was flanked by Chesapeake Bay on one side and Back River on the other. Hiking and biking trails, fishing opportunities and areas of historical interest made up the popular park, but at night the place was deserted.

As he made the turn onto Bay Shore Road, he shut off the headlights and slowed to a crawl.

"Can you tell me where we're going now?"

She was damn tired of being left in the dark, literally and figuratively. Though traffic wasn't an issue, running with his headlights off could prove problematic when one considered the wildlife flitting around in the park.

"There's an old deserted building near the bay," he explained.

Even though she'd heard him speak before and knew exactly what to expect, that deep voice made her shiver. She wanted to kick herself.

"The child is supposed to be there," he went on.

This was crazy. "You expect me to believe that it's going to be that easy. The kidnapper just left her there for you to pick up?" She wished for her firearm. Not that she'd seen any indication that he was armed. Still, she liked this less and less with each passing minute.

He made the final turn that would lead them to their destination. "I've told you all I know."

She thought she was prepared for his next move, but she wasn't. He stopped the SUV, shifted into Park and shut off the ignition, then turned to her. "This is a trap. Set by whom, I don't know. Why, I don't know. But I know it for what it is." He looked forward, into the darkness. "I'm going in there. If anything goes wrong, I want you to call your friend Agent Lewis. But don't do anything unless absolutely necessary. The important thing here is making sure the child is safe."

Ann got it now; she was the eyewitness. Whatever happened, someone had to be able to explain the events and how they unfolded. He could pretend it was about the child all he wanted to, but she wasn't so sure. She shook her head. "This is a bad idea." She studied the outline of the old building that backed up to the bay in the distance. "A very bad idea."

"Yeah." His gaze met hers once more. "But unless you have a better proposal, this is the plan."

No way. She reached for her cell phone. "I'm calling Lewis now." Whatever this guy was up to, she wasn't going to let this go any further. Instinct was screaming at her to do something.

To call backup.

He grabbed her hand but didn't attempt to take the phone away from her. "Just do what I asked. If I'm not back in five minutes or if you have reason to suspect trouble, make the call."

Trouble? She already suspected trouble. She stared out at the building again. But what if the child was in there? What if someone was watching, waiting for his orders to be followed?

"I can't do this," she argued as she pulled her hand free of his. "If that little girl is in there, too many things could go wrong. We don't have enough information to move forward with this strategy."

"Whoever is behind these kidnappings," he fired back, "asked for me, only me. I can't risk the child's safety by failing to do exactly as I was told."

A bark of laughter, motivated by her rising panic, burst from her throat. "I'm sorry. The news reports on how you bust in and execute the bad guys to rescue an endangered child in each scenario. If you're really who you want me to believe you are, where's your plan?" Maybe she'd said too much, but this wasn't the time to be less than honest.

"This is different."

"No kidding."

He pinned her with an icy glare that cut right through the darkness. "This is not my game, Ms. Martin. Someone else is making the rules. Now get behind the wheel and be prepared to do whatever you have to."

Before she could say more, he got out and headed for the building.

Ann climbed across the console, gripped her cell phone tightly and fought the urge to enter Lewis's number. He'd told her to wait. Whoever the hell *he* was.

Five minutes. She glanced at the digital display on the dash. He had five minutes and then she was calling for backup.

She squinted, tried to make him out as he moved toward the building, but he'd already melted into the darkness.

Two minutes passed. Then three. Her pulse whipped into overdrive. Two more minutes and she was making that call. The anticipation building, she checked her phone to ensure service was strong. All bars were in place. Nothing to worry about there.

One more minute.

She opened her phone, prepared to press the speed-dial number for Lewis.

And the last thing she'd expected to happen did....

The man wearing the baseball cap was out of the building and moving toward the SUV again. In his arms was a little girl with long dark hair.

"Oh...my...God."

He really was the Guardian Angel.

Chapter Nine

4:55 a.m.

"The pickup has been accomplished, Mr. Kendall."

Kendall's personal assistant, Owen Johnson, pointed to the monitor where special cameras with night-recording capabilities followed the movements of a man wearing a baseball cap.

Owen tapped the screen. "It's him," he said knowingly. "He's taking the child out of the building. He isn't wearing gloves this time. We should get the transmission of his fingerprints any moment now."

Phillip Kendall leaned back in his luxurious leather chair and watched as the child was carried to the SUV by the unidentified man known as the

Guardian Angel. He was quite tall, six-two, perhaps. Lean frame but, from all reports, quite strong.

The “Guardian Angel.” Savior of children. A hero, the media called him.

Fury knotted in Phillips’s gut. The man was a killer.

“I’ve seen enough.”

Owen darkened the monitor and turned to his boss. “Shall we follow him? He may lead us right to his own front door.”

“No, don’t follow him,” Phillip countered, surprising the other man. “He’ll come to us each time he is issued an invitation.” There were things Phillip wanted to know before he captured his prey. Things that would make the endgame so much more exciting.

This mystery man known as the Guardian Angel served as judge, jury and executioner whenever he performed his miraculous rescues. More often than not, the children were the sole survivors of his one-man rescue operations. He never left a print. Never. Didn’t leave a single trace of evidence. Not even a lone strand of hair. The idea that he was not wearing gloves on this occasion struck Phillip as peculiar.

Fury abruptly mushroomed inside him. He wanted to know all there was to know about this man and then he wanted *him.* Phillip wanted to personally see to his execution. He didn't deserve to breathe a moment longer than necessary. His death would be slow and painful. Very painful.

The world considered this bastard to be a hero for saving those children from the likes of drug-addicted pedophiles. No one realized that in his lofty pursuit he had murdered an innocent man for being in the wrong place at the wrong time. No one recognized that the Guardian Angel was no better than the scum he executed. Like his victims, he should be tried and proper punishment carried out in one efficient swoop.

Phillip's son hadn't deserved to die. Bad timing—that was all that had placed him in harm's way. A misunderstanding that should not have happened. And now someone had to pay.

Phillip could have taken care of everything. But he hadn't gotten the chance to make things right. Hadn't gotten the opportunity to prove he was a good father. That was the worst travesty of all.

He had only just found his son. They had barely gotten to know each other and this bastard took him away. Renewed rage detonated inside him. He would pay. Phillip would see that he paid in the worst way.

"Find out who he is, Owen. I want to know everything. Then I want him to stand before me and face the consequences of his actions."

"I understand, sir."

There was no need to be concerned about following him just yet. Phillip would know who he was. He would know what this Guardian Angel held near to his heart.

And then Phillip would take it away right before his eyes. Then he would die a slow, agonizing death for the murder of an innocent…but only after he had suffered sufficiently.

Phillip considered that thought a moment. What was the going price for an only son?

Phillip wasn't worried. It would come to him.

"Wait," he announced, halting Owen's exit. "Let's move up the timeline. I want the next child put into position within the coming twenty-four hours. I want this bastard." He hesitated, savored the thought. "Find out all you can about the woman, as well. I want to know why he would dare trust her."

Hesitation flashed in his personal assistant's eyes. "You're certain about moving up the timeline, sir? If we move too hastily we—"

"Yes, quite certain," Phillip said pointedly, cutting off his arguments. He did not like his orders questioned. "This time don't make it so easy for him. He might as well start paying now."

Owen nodded, his expression solemn. "Yes, sir."

He was worried. But Phillip was not. Wasn't that why he was rich? No one was better at predicting the deepest, darkest desires of others. He'd made his fortune a dozen times over using that uncanny instinct.

That same instinct was screaming at him now. He had to punish this man no matter the cost or the risk. He would not fail.

He had taken the one thing Phillip loved most. No matter how long it took, *he* would pay.

He would pay many times over.

Chapter Ten

7:30 a.m.

The throb of blue lights sliced through the gray dawn, the repetitive flicker making Ann's head hurt worse. She shouldn't have a headache or the twist in her gut.

Kira Robbins was safe.

This was outstanding news.

So far, there was no indication that any sort of harm had been done to the child other than the fear and worry that she might never again see her parents. The initial interview suggested that she had been properly fed and sheltered.

Her clothing, even her skin, had been scanned for prints and any detectable trace material. The full results wouldn't be available for several more hours, but the initial findings were not encouraging as far as potential evidence was concerned.

The really bad news was that the little girl couldn't provide any details about her captors. The person who'd fed her wore a mask and never spoke. The room had been dark. There'd been no sound. No smells she could recall. Nothing.

"We're through here."

Ann snapped from her thoughts and settled her attention on Agent Frank Lewis. He was not happy with her. Not happy at all.

"Good." She needed a conference call with Victoria to update her on this turn of events.

Ann climbed into Lewis's sedan. The SUV she'd driven to the E.R. was being processed by Forensics. The assumption was that it belonged to *him*. The Guardian Angel.

"This doesn't look good, Ann," Lewis said when they had rolled past the police roadblock where Bay Shore Road intersected North Point Road.

The Bureau was extremely unhappy with her all the way around. Felt just like old times.

"I don't know what you want me to say, Lewis." They'd been over last night's events three times. She had told him all there was to tell. "Blue eyes, dark hair, long, past his shoulders, secured in a ponytail. Tall, six-two, maybe. Lean frame."

The answering silence went on a few seconds too long. He didn't believe her. She would be the first to admit that the whole story sounded pretty damned preposterous, but it was the truth.

"You didn't get enough facial detail to work with a sketch artist?"

He didn't bother trying to hide the skepticism in his tone. The fact that he'd asked that question already confirmed her suspicion that he thought she was being less than truthful with him.

"I can try, Lewis, but about all I can adequately describe is the jawline." She didn't see the point in mentioning the lips. The reality was, her mind was still spinning from the whole episode.

When he'd stepped from that building with the little girl in his arms, she'd stopped being an investigator. She'd suddenly felt nine years old and at a total loss for what to do next. He'd handed the child to her and told her to go. Then he'd disappeared into the night.

She should have tried to stop him. She should have demanded answers. But she hadn't. She'd watched him walk away and then she'd done exactly what he told her—driven to the nearest hospital. Calling Lewis en route had ensured that the agent had arrived within minutes of her reaching the hospital.

Once the child's condition had been confirmed as good and the parents were on the scene, the questions had begun in earnest. The Bureau as well as the local cops were more than a little suspicious of her story. Not that she could blame either. The entire event had one hell of a fantasy feel. She was reasonably sure she wouldn't have believed it herself had she not been there.

"One of our agents delivered your rental to your hotel."

"Thanks." Ann closed her eyes and tried to slow the pounding in her skull.

"You realize just how off-the-wall this sounds," Lewis said. Not a question, a statement.

The answer was yes; but then, he knew that. "I can only repeat what happened," she said again. "He showed up. Told me he'd gotten a message about the girl's location. He drove me to the park. The kid was there. End of story."

Lewis slowed for a stop sign. "Except that's not where the story ended."

Ann exhaled a lungful of frustration. How many times were they going to go over this? "What was I supposed to do? Leave the kid in the SUV and follow him? I wasn't armed. It's not like I could have stopped him from taking off." She studied his profile. "The Bureau's position on the matter should be about the child. Kira Robbins is alive and back with her parents. That's a major accomplishment, Agent."

"The Bureau wants this guy, Ann," Lewis said bluntly. "You might consider him a big hero right now, but he's killed six people. The fact that they were all criminals is not the point. The vigilantism has to stop. The media is eating this up. How many more wannabe heroes will take up arms and mimic his actions?"

She was well aware of all those things. Until a few hours ago she would have said the same, but something had shifted deep inside her when he'd handed that child to her. The past, she recognized, was interfering with her ability to look at the incident from a rational standpoint. Unfortunately, the past was part of who she was, good, bad or indifferent.

What Lewis said was true. But this was no longer merely about the Guardian Angel. There were five other children missing in the Fear Factor case. If the unknown subjects responsible for those abductions were playing some kind of game with the man she met last night, then she and everyone else involved in this investigation had to step back and see where this went. The other children's lives could be at stake.

Any wrong moves or mistakes on their part

could adversely affect the momentum of this case. It was impossible to assess an unknown enemy. Risk management didn't exist in a situation where there were only variables and no solid facts.

"The crime scene was too clean," Lewis said, not telling her anything she didn't already know.

"I didn't see or hear anyone," she repeated the statement she had already made to both Lewis and the deputy representing the sheriff's department. "If there was any evidence in the vicinity, it was cleaned up *after* I left with the girl."

"This Guardian Angel believes someone is attempting to set him up?" Lewis asked.

She'd answered that question twice already, as well. "Yes." She pinned him with a look as he braked at an intersection. "He's certain someone is setting him up, but he doesn't have any idea who or why."

Lewis shook his head, cut her a look. "I'm not buying the idea that the unsubs behind Fear Factor went to all that trouble just to set up this guy."

"What about the Bureau?"

More of that stinging silence radiated inside the vehicle before he said, "You think we know where those children are and that we're allowing the parents to endure hell while we try and reel in a vigilante?" He pulled out onto 695. "You've gotta be kidding, Ann."

Leaning fully into the seat, she closed her eyes. Of course she wasn't suggesting that the Bureau was keeping the children away from their parents any more than she was that they were behind the abductions. She did, however, know just how badly they wanted to nail the guy. The need to get the situation under control could very well adversely affect the way the investigation was conducted. To think otherwise was illogical. She'd had almost the same training, though attained on the job, as Lewis. He could rationalize the Bureau's objectives all he wanted to, but facts were facts.

"Don't put words in my mouth, Lewis." Dawn had broken. "Whoever this guy is, Fear Factor is connected to him on some level."

"Or maybe he's responsible for the Fear Factor abductions." Lewis pushed the speed limit, headed back into Baltimore proper.

"Maybe." She couldn't deny that she had considered the same theory. The idea that someone had given him the location of the child was just too out-there to be a coincidence. "But he's been rescuing children—if the legends can be believed—for years without having to drum up his own victims."

That theory just didn't cut it for her. Not anymore. It wasn't as though he needed any extra buildup in the media. They already ate up his every move. There simply wasn't a logical motive for that action. No motive, no action. Basic investigative work.

"If this was a trap," Lewis offered, "why didn't whoever is supposedly setting him up move in? Why just let him walk away?"

Another question she couldn't answer.

"We figure that out—" she turned toward him "—we'll solve this case." She was convinced that the answers lay right there—with the Guardian Angel. "I need a few hours' sleep," she warned. "I'll come in later and work with your sketch artist if you think it'll help."

"It wouldn't hurt to scan a few databases, review the photos. See if anyone pops out at you. Who knows—one of the faces might trigger a memory."

That was assuming their guy had a record. She had a feeling he didn't. He'd gone about his business without the use of gloves. If he was worried about being tagged, he'd shown no indications.

There simply was no cut-and-dried answer to any of this. A complicated, multitiered mystery—the man and the events playing out.

Lewis fished his cell phone from his pocket. "Lewis."

A couple of yeses and an "I understand" made up his end of the conversation. When he closed the phone and shoved it back into his pocket, he glanced at her. "The SUV was a dead end. The prints we believe to be his don't match anything in any of our databases."

The urge to smile tugged at her lips, but she resisted. What was this guy up to? How the hell had her aversion for his acts turned to admiration so damned fast? "Still nothing at the scene?"

"Nothing yet. They started another sweep as soon as it was daylight to ensure nothing was missed."

But they wouldn't find anything significant. She was certain of little in this case, but that was one thing she felt quite positive about.

The only way they were gong to identify the Guardian Angel was if he chose to reveal himself. As for the unsubs involved in Fear Factor, that part was still very unclear to her. Large ransoms had been collected for those children. Why just let them go using one or more for baiting a media-created celebrity? The children were worth far too much as salable commodities. If money was the goal, why throw away potential additional profits?

There were a lot of very sick people in this world, and it never really surprised her what some were willing to do in order to accomplish their goals. Maybe Fear Factor was one of those scenarios.

Another call came in on Lewis's cell. A single "I understand" was his only response this time. His gaze connected with hers again as he dropped the phone back into his pocket. "Katherine Fowler and her husband are waiting for you at your hotel."

She should have anticipated that reaction to the news. "What can I tell them?" Might as well find out how much leeway she had before being faced with questions.

"There's really not much to tell," he offered. His lips twisted wryly. "We don't have any evidence. We don't have anything but unproven theories on what happened last night."

"I can tell her about Guardian Angel?" That was the part that would interest Katherine Fowler the most. *He* had answered her plea for help.

Or had he been reacting to the summons of another source?

"Keep it vague," Lewis cautioned.

As if what she knew was anything *but* vague. "Well, at least that part will be easy."

Vague was a perfect description for what they had.

"I need some guarantee from you that the next time he contacts you," Lewis said, the suspicion missing from his tone now, "you'll inform me immediately."

She avoided looking in Lewis's direction. She couldn't make him that promise. The circumstances would dictate her actions.

"I'll do my best." She thought about the man with the baseball cap. "There's no guarantee he'll contact me again," she warned.

"He'll contact you," Lewis countered. "You're his only link to this case."

Maybe.

If she were damned lucky.

If the children were lucky.

Chapter Eleven

8:40 a.m.

Trey Fowler was uncharacteristically reticent for a man who hadn't wanted Ann involved in the investigation to find his daughter. She'd expected him to rant about how her involvement could have backfired—could still backfire.

"Give me your gut feeling," Katherine Fowler urged. She stood in the center of Ann's hotel room, her hands clasped tightly in front of her. "I need to hear good news, Ms. Martin."

Ann's heart went out to the woman. She wanted her daughter back, would give anything to make it happen. An ancient memory attempted to intrude on Ann's focus. Her own mother looking pale and heartsick. Ann pushed it away. This case had nothing to do with her past.

"Mrs. Fowler, I can't promise you that your daughter will be released in a similar manner." The woman's face visibly fell. "But I can say without reservation that if the unsub's motive is to somehow trap this man known as the Guardian Angel, then logic would dictate that another child and then another might be used for that purpose." She chose not to use the word *bait*.

"Who is this Guardian Angel?" Trey Fowler stepped into the conversation. Unlike his wife, his hands hung calmly at his sides and his face showed only grim resignation. "What does the Fear Factor case have to do with him?"

Frank Lewis, who had stayed out of the dialogue until now, shifted in his chair so that he could look directly at Trey Fowler. "We don't know the answer to that just yet, sir."

Ann was grateful Lewis had taken that question. Telling Fowler that she had no idea how to answer his questions would only have confirmed his belief that she didn't belong on this case.

Lewis glanced at her then. "At this point, Ms. Martin is our sole connection to this lead."

The impulse to stand and pace nudged Ann, but she kept her seat on the foot of the bed. Lewis had chosen one of the four chairs at the table. Though the room wasn't a suite, it did have a small sitting area that adequately suited the purposes of this meeting. The decision to sit had not been a conscious one, nor was it rude to do so when the Fowlers opted not to. She and Lewis had the same training. Taking a seat at a time like this was a way to inject calm into the situation. Even though the Fowlers refused to do the same, the effort on hers and Lewis's part provided a reassuring effect. Defusing the hysteria was essential.

Trey shoved the fingers of his right hand through his hair, the first sign of his insecurity. As brave as he wanted to appear, he was scared to death just like his wife. "This doesn't make any sense at all."

No kidding. Time to take charge of the moment. Ann pushed to her feet. "Mr. Fowler, there is every reason to believe that we'll hear from the Guardian Angel again."

Katherine Fowler's gaze locked on Ann's. "How can you be so sure?"

Ann glanced at Lewis. When he didn't give any indication that she shouldn't proceed, she offered, "If whoever is behind Fear Factor has some vendetta to settle with the Guardian Angel, we have to assume that he has a game plan that involves the children." Ann looked from Katherine to Trey. "The Bureau and the local police will continue to conduct their investigations as per proper protocol. And based on what happened last night, as Agent Lewis suggested, I believe this mystery man considers me his link to that investigation. I'm confident that I'll be hearing from him again."

Katherine searched Ann's face as if looking for some hint of promise. "Tell him I need my baby back," she pleaded. "I'll do anything to get her back. We have more money."

"Katherine," Trey cautioned. He put his arm around her waist, the movement stilted. "The Bureau is going to find our daughter."

Ann wished there was something she could say to assure Katherine, but she'd said all there was to say. "I'll do everything I can, Mrs. Fowler. You have my word." She supposed she should have directed her statement to Mr. Fowler, as well, but she understood that he still didn't care for her participation in this case. Still, not about to be deterred by his obvious disregard, Ann added, "The best news is that, considering Kira Robbins's release, there is every reason to believe that all the children are alive and as safe as they can be under the circumstances."

Katherine's lips trembled into a smile, and her eyes glittered with barely restrained tears. As horrific as this nightmare was, that part was something to be thankful about.

"Let's go, Katherine." Fowler ushered his wife toward the door. "Thank you, Agent Lewis." Fowler glanced at Ann. "Ms. Martin."

Ann refused to feel slighted by the man. He didn't want her here. Didn't want his wife depending upon someone outside the usual law enforcement channels. He'd just have to get over it since Ann wasn't going anywhere until she'd found Caroline Fowler.

Tell Katherine Fowler that I will find her child....

The so-called Guardian Angel had said he would find the children.

Ann hoped like hell he meant what he'd said, because right now he was the one and only link they had to those missing kids. And even that connection was mighty damn thin.

When the Fowlers were gone, Ann turned back to Lewis. "What kind of surveillance has been ordered?"

Lewis tried to sound surprised but didn't pull it off. He stood. "Surveillance on who?"

Ann held up both hands. He wasn't fooling her. "Don't even try to pull that one on me. I worked with you guys too long. I know how this goes down."

She was no longer on the periphery of this investigation; she was a person of interest to the case. Her every move would be monitored. She hadn't decided if she had a problem with that. Though she hadn't felt in actual danger in the Guardian Angel's presence, she was no fool. He was an unknown factor, another variable in an already shaky case.

Lewis sighed, a weary sound. "We have a couple of agents watching the entrances to the hotel. Your phone line is being monitored. Cell, too."

Great. "You must have a judge in your pocket to get a court order that fast."

His smile was halfhearted. "The Fowlers aren't exactly June and Ward Cleaver. You know that politics is the name of the game around here."

He wasn't kidding about that. Fatigue crushed down on Ann's shoulders. She needed some downtime. "I should call in to my office and then get some sleep."

Lewis nodded and headed for the door. "We're having a postmortem of the night's events in the director's office at three." He paused at the door. "You coming?"

"I'll be there."

He left the room, didn't look back. Ann locked the door behind him. She made the call to Victoria and brought her up to speed. Then she plugged her cell phone into the charger, showered, dressed and collapsed onto the bed.

Sleep.

She had to sleep.

And if she was damned lucky, she wouldn't dream.

RUN!

Ann couldn't stop. Had to keep running…or he *would find her.*

Hurry!

The pounding caused her to stumble. She fell face-first toward the ground.

More pounding.

Ann's eyes snapped open and she sat up.

"Damn it." She pushed the hair back from her face. Took stock of her surroundings. Hotel. Baltimore.

Just a dream. She inhaled a slow, deep breath, then another, forcing her heart rate to decelerate.

Same old dream.

Damn it.

She shook it off. Cleared her head. Had someone been knocking on her door or was that part of the damned dream, too? The drapes were pulled tight, leaving the room dimly lit. Eleven-fifteen in the morning. She'd only been asleep about an hour. She peered at the door. Locked. Chain in place. Had to be the dream. She looked again. Something white on the floor snagged her attention. Ann blinked to ensure she wasn't imagining it.

Envelope.

Kicking the cover aside, she scooted to the edge of the bed and pushed to her feet. She padded to the door, her bare feet silent on the carpet, and crouched down to take a look. White business-size envelope. *Ann Martin* was scrawled across the front. She picked up the envelope and moved back to the bed, then turned on the lamp. After rubbing the last of the sleep from her eyes with her thumb and forefinger, she opened the envelope and removed the single piece of plain white paper.

Three words were written on the page.

Unlock your door.

Her heart stumbled.

Ann folded the page and tucked it back into the envelope before shoving the whole thing into the drawer on the bedside table. She stood. Took another deep, calming breath and crossed the room. That her hands shook as she reached for the lock and chain annoyed her unreasonably. Hesitation delayed her before she slid the chain out of its channel.

She was unarmed. Her pepper spray was clear across the room.

But it was *him*—she knew it was him. He hadn't hurt her last night: chances were he wasn't going to now.

She released the chain, flipped the dead bolt and took two steps back. When the lever moved downward, she considered that she should have opened the drapes to allow the morning sun into the room. Should have fished her pepper spray from her purse just in case.

His overwhelming presence suddenly filled the space between her and the only exit. He let the door close behind him and locked it before settling his attention fully on her. The plain black cap was pulled low, as before. The black T-shirt and jeans the same as last night. She told herself to focus on details…other than his lips…but then he spoke and the effort was wasted.

"I received another message."

The smooth, deep sound of his voice had its impact a whole ten seconds before his words penetrated the stratum of surrealism his presence evoked.

"When?" The word came out breathless and fragile. She hated sounding weak. She wrestled away her trepidation and grabbed back her determination. "Delivered in the same manner as before?"

"Yes," he confirmed. "The message came via the same chat group. About an hour ago."

Anticipation pounded in her veins. "You have another location?"

He nodded. "Midnight tonight. Sherry Curtis will be waiting at the location specified."

Sherry Curtis, the second victim. This was utterly unbelievable. And yet exactly what she had hoped for. If the unsubs in this case continued to release the children, there was hope Caroline Fowler's turn would come.

Unless…whoever was behind this got what he wanted first.

Her attention fixed on the man standing inches away. She couldn't let that happen.

"Then someone wants you badly," she said, "but he's obviously not through playing games."

He met her eyes for the first time since coming into the room. "That would appear to be the case."

"Have you considered your enemies?" Might as well get down to business. Lewis had people watching the hotel. If this man had been seen entering, their time could be short. Part of her wanted to warn him. The other part—the more rational part—hoped the agents would close in and take this guy down. Trouble was, he didn't strike her as the sort of man who could be forced into cooperation. He would probably shut down and refuse to even talk if taken against his will.

If that happened, she could lose her one connection to the person or persons responsible for the missing children, including Caroline Fowler.

"I don't have any enemies, Ms. Martin."

A laugh burst from her throat, the sound a bit choked even as she tried to sound detached. "We all have enemies, Mr...." She searched his face, noting the details that she knew she would later recall in an altogether unprofessional way. "What am I supposed to call you?"

He stared at her with those piercing blue eyes for half a dozen crashes of her heart against her sternum. "Nathan. You can call me Nathan."

The name, his voice, combined with the way he looked at her, made speech increasingly difficult. Strange, she didn't once remember that happening to her. Had to be the whole mystery element cloaking him—the personification of good against evil...even if she didn't necessarily see it that way.

"So, Nathan, what about enemies? You killed six people. Somewhere along the way you've clearly ticked someone off."

"Each of those situations was self-defense," he

reminded her. "My goal was always to rescue the child, not to take vengeance. That's where the media gets it wrong. I'm not a vigilante."

The Bureau got it wrong, too, evidently. So had she. "Your remorse appears to be overwhelming."

The doubt that darkened his features made her wish she could take back the words. Too late for that.

"Don't expect me to regret protecting myself from the kind of scumbag who would hurt a child."

He was right about that part. She doubted a jury anywhere would convict him. *Focus.* This wasn't about him. It was about the children. Unlike the FBI, she was here for one client. "I say we start with determining each victim's next of kin and see what we come up with. A friend or family member may have decided to try going after you." Good starting place. "A list of anyone you've crossed, personally or professionally, would be useful, as well."

"Trust me, Ms. Martin," he urged softly but no less fiercely, "no one has a vendetta against me, personally or professionally."

How could he be so sure? Even the best person had stepped on the occasional toe, even if inadvertently. "But," she argued, the theory foremost in her mind her primary motivation, "someone may have hard feelings toward the Guardian Angel." She folded her arms over her chest. "And that's you. If your enemy had any doubts that you and the Guardian Angel were one and the same, you alleviated those last night when you picked up Kira Robbins."

"That's why I need you."

At least he was honest. "You know the Bureau is watching this hotel. My room phone as well as my cell is being monitored. I'm not sure I can help you without reporting the activity. Unlike you, I'm required to work within the boundaries of the law."

He searched her eyes a moment, then said, "I see. You're among those who call me a killer, is that it?" His gaze skimmed her from head to toe and back. "I didn't get that impression last night."

She couldn't halt the shiver that rushed over her skin. "I have no desire to argue legalities with you, Nathan," she returned bluntly. "If there's something I can do to bring the rest of those children home, that's what I need to be doing. So are we going to stand around here wasting time or are we going to do this?" If he wanted to take his chances with getting caught, that was fine by her, as long as her goal was the end result.

He considered her question for what felt like an eternity before saying, "We should leave now."

Easier said than done. "How do you propose we do that with federal agents watching both entrances?"

"We're back to that trust thing again, aren't we?"

Trust me, Ms. Martin....

Clearly he had a plan and expected her to just blindly follow. Okay, she could do that…for now. "I'll get my shoes."

Ann left him standing at the door. Thankfully she'd dressed in track pants and a pullover before hitting the sack. Tug on her shoes, run a brush through her hair, grab her cell and she'd be good to go.

Two minutes later and she was back at the door and ready to do this thing. She banished thoughts of how furious Lewis would be when he found out she'd been contacted again and hadn't let him know.

"How are we going to do this?" She wasn't going to operate completely in the dark. If he had a plan, she wanted to know the details.

"We'll leave the same way I arrived."

That told her nothing at all.

He checked the corridor before emerging from the room. She followed in spite of the lack of details. She wasn't surprised that he chose the stairwell over the elevator. His stealth was admirable. He scarcely made a sound. Even with all her training, she wasn't that good.

On the ground level he checked the corridor, then the lobby as they passed through. When he led her beyond a door marked Employees Only she realized his plan. Maintenance entrance. Would Lewis's people even think to watch that door?

That they didn't encounter any actual employees was either a well-planned strategy or sheer luck. He stopped near the double-door exit and retrieved a bag from behind a stack of boxes. He tossed a pair of white coveralls at her and reached into the bag for a second pair. She stepped into the coveralls, pulled them into place and slid the zipper upward. He did the same before pulling two white caps from the bag. The black one he usually wore went into the bag.

He settled his cap into place with his hair tucked inside it, picked up the bag and glanced in her direction. "This way."

He paused at the exit doors before opening one. "There's a white panel van outside. Climb into the passenger side and pick up the clipboard in the seat as if you're checking our next stop."

She nodded. Wouldn't matter if Lewis's colleagues were watching or not. No one was going to question maintenance coming in and out of the building. Nathan had thought out his plan thoroughly.

The white van displayed a logo for a popular heating-and-cooling provider. Once they were in the van, Nathan started the engine and pulled away from the side entrance. It wasn't until they had merged into traffic on the cross street that she asked any questions.

"Where are we going?" The idea that Lewis was going to make life very difficult for her kept skipping through her head. He was not going to be happy with this decision. But then, she had a history of decisions the Bureau didn't care for.

"My place."

Ann stared out at the noon traffic. His place? He was actually going to trust her with his full identity? The one professionally trained brain cell still operating at full capacity warned that she should be worried, nervous at the very least. But she wasn't. He was it—her one chance at finding Caroline Fowler and the other four children still missing.

She was taking the chance.

Victoria had warned her to use extreme caution

when dealing with this enigma. Lewis had ordered her to let him know if there was any contact. Ann had done neither.

She couldn't worry about the latter; she had to roll with this, couldn't risk altering the momentum. In just a few hours another child would be released. If the unsubs holding those children suspected trouble, one or more of the children could be harmed. The contact could abruptly stop. She couldn't take that risk.

All she could do was play by the rules thrown at her.

The driver braked for a traffic signal. "Look in the glove box."

She shot him a questioning glance.

"There's a blindfold," he explained. "I'll need you to put that on."

She laughed. "You're kidding, right?"

One look into those icy blue eyes and she knew he wasn't.

"Whatever." She opened the glove box and took out a pair of eye covers, the kind used for blocking light when sleeping. Once the eye covers were in place, she asked, "Happy now?" These were the really good kind. She couldn't see a damned thing.

"Grab the lever on the side of your seat and adjust the seat into a full recline," he said then.

"We don't want to attract any unnecessary attention."

She released a frustrated breath, ensuring the sound conveyed her impatience with his ridiculous request.

To add another layer of frustration, he turned on the radio, pumped up the volume so listening to the traffic sounds was impossible.

The minutes felt like hours, with her patience running thinner and thinner. She reminded herself that she was doing this for the children. Then she remembered the postmortem at three.

"Hey."

When the volume on the radio was lowered, she said, "I have a meeting downtown with Agent Lewis and his director at three."

"That's a meeting I'm afraid you'll have to miss."

"Wait." She reached up to remove the blindfold, simultaneously pushing into an upright position.

"Don't move, Ms. Martin," he warned. The timbre of his voice told her that he was dead serious. "Keep the blindfold in place."

She lowered her hand back to her waist and considered her limited options. "This meeting is part of the strategy for this investigation, Nathan. It's important that I'm there."

Silence.

"Are you listening to me?" This was no time for him to go psycho control freak on her. During the protracted moment that followed her demand she started to seriously question her initial assessment of this guy. She was rarely wrong, but there was always a first time and this could definitely be that time. She needed him to think, to look past what he knew and anticipate the possibilities.

"Do you believe," he finally offered, "that anything revealed or decided in this meeting will help you crack this case or discover the location of the remaining children?"

That wasn't a fair question. "It's impossible for me to predict what the Bureau may have found between this morning and now. There might have been evidence recovered from the park. There could be a break in the case anytime. And if I'm not at the three-o'clock briefing, I won't get those details."

"There won't be a break in the case."

That he stated this with such certainty set her on edge.

"How can you be so sure?" The idea that some folks at the Bureau theorized that Guardian Angel was behind these abductions trickled into her thoughts.

"Because this isn't about the money or the

children, Ms. Martin. This is about me. I thought we had established that already."

For the most part, she agreed with his conclusion. But that didn't mean she planned to ignore the rest of the investigation. The Bureau had top profilers working on every aspect of this case.

She altered her strategy. "Besides, you know if I'm not there, they'll come looking for me."

"Don't worry," he said, his voice eerily soft. "They won't be able to find you."

Chapter Twelve

"You may remove the blindfold."

Nathan had never brought anyone to his home. Well, no one outside Addison, his agent and PR rep, and Charles, his houseman. This hasty decision could prove a monumental mistake. But he didn't think so.

She was like him.

He sensed it in every fiber of his being.

She removed the covering from her eyes and blinked to focus. He'd led her from the garage through the mudroom and into his kitchen. She took stock of her surroundings, then leveled her gaze on his.

"Nice place."

A smile pulled at his lips. He had known she would make a nonchalant comment such as that.

"You should eat," he announced. "Then we'll talk."

She glanced around the room. "I'm okay." Her gaze landed on his once more. "Let's talk now."

He had also expected that reaction.

"Have a drink first," he insisted. "There's a variety of nonalcoholic beverages in the fridge. I'll return shortly."

He left the kitchen before she could question him. It was safe to leave her alone for the moment. The security system was armed. She could not leave the house, and Charles was already gone for the day. Charles arrived early each morning; by ten his time was done. He had been in Nathan's employ for a decade. A more loyal and dedicated human being would not be found.

Nathan went to his office and checked the monitors that remained on 24-7. No new AMBER Alerts. He skimmed the police log for the past eight hours. Nothing for him. He pulled up the map he'd been considering in the wee hours of the morning and sent the diagram to the printer. Before entering discussions with Ann Martin, he needed to be armed with this meager evidence. Taking it with him to her hotel would have been too risky. As careful as he was, there was always a chance he would fail.

When the page ejected, he marked each Baltimore location at which he had rescued a child in the past two years. Six altogether. Then he highlighted the park where they had found Kira Robbins before dawn this morning and the old abandoned school building where Sherry Curtis would supposedly be at midnight.

Each of the two locations coincided with a rescue he had orchestrated. By tomorrow the FBI would recognize that, as well, and this game would become far more difficult to anticipate.

Whoever was behind this illogical scheme had gone to a lot of trouble to set up this baiting game. Why not take Nathan or, at the very least, confront him last night when he picked up the Robbins girl? What was the point of repeating the step tonight?

There had to be a point.

Ann Martin was more right than she knew. He had himself an enemy related to his Guardian Angel activities. As she suggested, he had considered the next of kin and close associates for each perpetrator he'd left dead at a scene. None had the means or the intelligence level to pull off something anywhere near as elaborate as this. He'd also considered key personnel at the Bureau, but he had ruled out each member.

That left him back at square one.

Half a million dollars' ransom had been paid for each child. Three million dollars in total. And yet he knew with complete certainty that this game was not about the money.

The screen monitoring Ann Martin's movements drew his attention. She had looked over the drink selection without choosing anything and was now wandering out of his kitchen to explore her surroundings.

He watched her with growing curiosity. His too-avid interest was an error in judgment. He knew this, but he simply couldn't help himself. Rarely did anyone intrigue him so. She had grown up in Baltimore. Been educated there. An honor student who'd turned down an invitation to become a special agent with the FBI. Instead she had worked as a freelance advisor in her capacity as an electronic-banking specialist.

Her whole life was the picture of abundant opportunities and happiness. Except for one twenty-four-hour period when she had been nine years old.

For twenty-four hours little Ann Martin had been missing. But then she had been found wandering in the woods near her family's lake house. No harm, no foul. Ann had checked out fine other than having been scared to death after a night in the woods alone.

Except that it hadn't been fine. Nathan understood that even if no one else could see it. Something tragic had happened to Ann during that twenty-four-hour period. Something only she knew about. He saw it in her eyes, heard it in her passion for finding the missing daughter of Katherine and Trey Fowler.

She had a secret that haunted her, kept her single and uncommitted.

He knew that place intimately.

For the first time in his life he wanted to know another human being that intimately.

If he were genuinely lucky, this desire would not prove to be the biggest mistake of his adult life.

THE HOUSE WAS massive.

Whatever this guy did for a living, he was doing it right.

Then again, this was obviously a historic home. Perhaps he had inherited well.

Ann roamed out of the enormous kitchen and into a corridor that led into a majestic entry hall.

"Wow." She turned all the way around, admiring the artwork and tapestries. Her attention settled on the towering front door, and she went directly to it, checked to see if it was locked. Of course it was.

"You surely don't want to leave so soon?"

She whipped around at the sound of his voice. It was then that she realized how perfectly he fit into this setting. The long, dark hair and compelling features reminded her of a Renaissance prince—one bent on conquering all enemies. The stories she'd loved as a kid about vampires and pirates flitted through her mind on the heels of that thought. He could handle the part of either quite well. Before she could stop the reaction, she shivered with something that she refused to confess and that was not at all akin to fear.

He watched her so closely, as if he could sense her uneasiness…an uneasiness complicated by attraction and desire.

Very strange that he could elicit such an unexpected blend of emotions from her.

"You trust me with your name and face but not with your address?" Didn't make a lot of sense to her. Unless he was that sure of the security of his identity.

He moved closer. "As I said before, you won't find me in any of your databases. But here—" he opened his arms wide as if to indicate all that surrounded him "—you can always find me."

She wasn't going to push the issue. He would either tell her who he was or he wouldn't. There were more pressing issues at the moment. Her attention settled on the paper in his hand and her anticipation spiked. "You have something to show me?"

"This way."

He led the way to what appeared to be his office. Massive desk, conference table and dozens of monitors. Four of the monitors were set to various news channels, the sound muted. Another monitored the rise and fall of stocks. The rest were in screen-saver mode.

Whatever this guy did, he liked keeping up with the world around him.

He placed the single sheet of paper on a clear spot on his desk. A map of the East Coast focused on the Baltimore area.

"These are the locations," he said as he touched several circled places on the map, "where I've rescued children over the past two years."

She remembered the press coverage from more than one of the locations. "And the two highlighted locations?" She recognized one as the park where Kira Robbins had been found.

"I'm sure you know that one," he suggested as he tapped the symbol representing the park.

"Yes."

"This—" he indicated the other highlighted area "—is where we'll find Sherry Curtis."

If Ann had harbored any doubt, with regard to this unsub's motive, she had none now. The person or persons behind Fear Factor were obsessed with the Guardian Angel—Nathan.

Her gaze met his. "You know that once you make this pickup tonight the Bureau will figure this out, too." She stared at the map once more. "If they haven't already." The profilers would run known facts about the park six ways to Sunday. The connection to the Guardian Angel rescue might be looked at as coincidence for the moment, but it certainly would not be ignored.

After tonight—assuming he walked away with the kid, as before—not only would the unsub be setting a trap for him, the Bureau would, as well. If a third child was released in this same method, both parties would be prepared for his arrival on the scene.

"You know what the Bureau will do." Maybe she shouldn't have said as much out loud, but this guy was no fool. He had to understand what he was up against. This was a no-win situation. To save the child he had to follow instructions, and doing that meant putting himself on the line with the good guys as well as the bad ones.

Ann had to perform a quick reality check. A true storybook hero just wasn't found anymore. Unless—her attention locked fully on her host—he was the real McCoy. She sure as hell had never run upon one.

For several seconds he searched her eyes as if attempting to determine if he could trust her completely with what he had to say next. "That's where you come in," he said, sending her trepidation to a whole new level.

Disbelief whirred along her nerve endings. "You're asking me to work against the Bureau?" She shook her head. "I can't do that."

"Then we'll be lucky to get the second child back, and any hope of retrieving the others will be lost."

The hell of it was he was right. Assuming the game continued to play out in the manner it had so far, the Bureau would get wise to the strategy and an ambush would be ready and waiting the next go-around. Unfortunately, the only good that would come from Nathan's arrest would be serving the Bureau's ego.

Ann took a mental step back. She knew the

law, respected her Bureau colleagues. But *this* had to be about finding those children—in particular, Caroline Fowler. That was her assignment.

"So what do you need me to do?"

Nathan hadn't expected her to cooperate quite so readily. The possibility that her agreement was a ruse barged into his thoughts, reminding him how easily this could go very, very wrong. But he had to trust her; he really had no choice.

He considered her question and came to the only logical conclusion. "You attend that three-o'clock meeting and you make sure your colleagues at the Bureau have no idea how tonight will go down. If necessary, persuade them not to consider that theory."

"I thought I was going to miss that meeting," she countered.

"If you're going for the benefit of the children, then, by all means, go." He held her gaze, knew he'd thrown down a gauntlet.

Uncertainty or maybe disbelief flashed in her eyes. He was asking a hell of a lot. To her credit, she quickly dismissed the uncertain emotion. "On one condition."

The challenge in her voice surprised him. The lady was definitely nobody's fool. Nor was she a coward. "What's that?"

"I'm there with you tonight. No arguments. I want in on all the details." She took a breath. "And I'll need to be armed."

Her requests were reasonable. The latter made his lips quirk with the need to smile—something few people were able to make him do. "You mean with something besides your pepper spray?"

Indignation made a brief appearance. "Yes, that's precisely what I mean."

"Come with me." Nathan led the way to the entry hall. Next to the closet door was the entry to the basement. "I have everything we'll need."

He opened the door, pushed the light switch into the on position and started down the narrow stairs. She hesitated on the first step. Not that he could blame her. There was a time when he wouldn't have gone into a basement for anything.

All that was behind him now…had been for years. He wasn't afraid of anything anyone could do to him. The only time he experienced fear was when the rescue of a child went wrong.

Nothing anyone could do to him personally could hurt him.

Not anymore.

Halfway down the flight of steps he paused, glanced back at her. "You coming?"

She lifted her chin a little higher as if defying her own fears. "Yeah. Sure."

At the bottom of the stairs he flipped another switch, flooding the large below-ground-level room with light. The glass doors of the locked cabinets lining the wall displayed most any kind of weapon one might need. Another vault-type cabinet housed the ammunition. Any supplies or gear he might need for mountain climbing, cross-country hiking or simply taking down an enemy was here in this large space.

"Are you planning to start a war?"

The astonishment in her voice as she asked the question forced the corners of his mouth upward once more. He'd never met anyone who could prompt that reaction from him so easily. "I'm a peaceful man by nature," he countered. "It's only when a child's safety is at risk that my warrior side surfaces."

Her gaze lingered on him a moment before she turned her attention to one cabinet in particular. She approached the weapons stored there with visible admiration.

"I'll take the forty-cal Glock." Her interest slid to him again. "Unless that's your weapon of choice."

He pulled the key from his pocket and unlocked

the cabinet. "I use a number of weapons. They all have their finer points."

He removed the Glock and passed the weapon to her. She weighed it with her right hand, then nodded her approval.

"This'll work."

The ammunition vault was his next stop. He provided her with the necessary ammo. "That should cover your needs."

She dropped the ammo into her purse and let the Glock hang at her side. "If I'm going to make that meeting, I should get back to my hotel and change."

There were many reasons why he shouldn't trust her. At the very top of the list was the idea that she was more cop than she was private investigator, no matter how she wanted to believe otherwise. Her years working in an advisory capacity with the Bureau had ensured that, at heart, blue steel ran through her veins. But she'd given him her word. He needed her. He had to trust her.

He locked the vault before allowing his eyes to meet hers once more. "You should eat first."

Not waiting for her to argue, he headed back upstairs. She followed without protest. He was sure she hadn't eaten and he needed her alert, at the top of her game.

It would take both of them to make this happen.

She placed her purse and weapon on the counter, then looked around the kitchen. "Has this house been in your family for generations?"

Ah, she was curious. He'd expected her curiosity to make an appearance eventually. He just hadn't anticipated it would be about his home.

"No." He reached into the fridge for sandwich fixings. Ham, turkey, cheese—he set all three on the counter and turned back to the fridge for condiments. "I bought the property ten years ago."

She surveyed the large room again. "Big house for a single guy."

Now she was fishing.

He focused on preparing the sandwiches for the next couple of minutes. She wandered around the room, sliding her hand over the granite counter, admiring the ornate woodwork of the cabinets and the richness of the limestone floors. None of which he could take credit for. Charles, his houseman, had contracted an interior decorator to bring the dilapidated home back to some semblance of grandeur. How anyone could allow a historical home such as this one to fall into disrepair was beyond Nathan's comprehension. As a child, he'd never dreamed he would own such a lavish home. Now that he did, he didn't take any part of it for granted.

He placed each sandwich on a plate and added chips. After setting one before her, he rummaged in the fridge once more for drinks. Designer bottled water. Nathan gave his head a little shake. Charles insisted on buying only the best. The way Nathan saw it, water was water.

"Have you always lived in Baltimore?"

Ah, more trolling for answers. He passed her a chilled bottle. "Who says we're in Baltimore?"

She considered his comment as she bit into her sandwich. When she had swallowed, she offered, "You're right. We were on the road long enough to have driven to Georgetown…." She took a deep breath. "Or maybe Annapolis."

He schooled his expression, ensuring no telltale reaction to her suggestions. "The less you know about me, the better." Even before he made the statement he realized she would not agree.

"That's a cop-out, partner."

She was right.

She nibbled on a chip. "You know a lot more about me than I know about you. It's difficult to work with that." She shrugged. "You want me to trust you, but you don't trust me."

So she'd moved on to a more psychological tactic. Touché.

"I'll make a deal with you, Ms. Martin," he

began, a part of him recognizing that he was more likely than not making a mistake.

"Ann," she interrupted. "Call me Ann."

How long had it been since he'd had an intimate conversation like this with a woman? He couldn't even remember. Relationships, even short-term ones, were complicated. Complications were something he could do without. He knew what he was about to do was an error in strategy even now and yet he couldn't resist.

"Ann," he acquiesced. "You can ask me one question if I can ask you one."

She wasn't fast enough to stifle the curiosity that flashed in her eyes. The offer was intriguing. The question was did she want information about him badly enough to give away some of her own?

"All right, I go first." She squared her shoulders in challenge. "Do we have a deal?"

"Deal." He took a bite of his sandwich.

"Why is your identity off-limits? Not just to me," she qualified. "To anyone, apparently."

She certainly hadn't wasted her one question. She'd made her query in such a way that responding would require giving away more than he'd hoped.

"I'm a very private man," he confessed. "My reasons are simple. I didn't like who I once was so I became someone else. The only way to ensure my old identity doesn't get mixed up with my new one is to keep them both close to the vest. The less information people know, the fewer questions they'll ask."

She pushed her plate away as if she'd lost her appetite. "That certainly answers the question," she groused, "but tells me nothing at all."

"The deal was," he reminded her, "you get one question, I get one question.

He had her there. "So what's your question?" The idea of him asking a personal question had sent her senses on alert. Her decision had clearly been a hasty one.

And then she knew the question. She saw it in his eyes even before he said the words.

"What happened to you when you were a little girl that you work so hard even now to pretend it didn't happen?"

The blood chilled in her veins despite the fact that she had known the question was coming. Memories flashed in her mind's eye, but she banished the ugly images. He was right about one thing: she worked hard, very hard, to forget that part of her past. She didn't talk about it. She wouldn't talk about it now.

Not for him...not for anyone.

"When I was nine," she began, her voice stilted despite her best efforts to keep it smooth, "I got lost in the woods near my parents' lake house. I wasn't found for more than twenty-four hours." She infused indifference into her tone. "But I was fine. A little terrified but fine."

He knew she was lying. She could see the confirmation of that conclusion in his eyes.

"Twenty-four hours is a long time in the eyes of a nine-year-old," he commented. "A lot can happen in that time."

She started to sweat. The nervous film instantly slicked her skin. "You had your question," she reminded him. If he thought she was saying any more, he could forget it. She was done with this game.

Why didn't he stop looking at her that way… as if he knew? He couldn't possibly know. No one knew.

"There are a lot of really bad people out there, Ann," he offered quietly. "Sometimes they're family, sometimes good friends. But we're not responsible for their actions when they hurt us."

Outrage chased away the anxious feelings. He didn't know a damn thing about her. This conversation was over! Way over. "Are you speaking from personal experience, Nathan? If not, then you might as well move past the subject, because that's all I have to say."

He held her gaze for what felt like a full minute, then confirmed, "Yes. I am speaking from personal experience."

She tried not to be affected by his admission. She really, really worked at not caring that his voice was stark with remembered pain.

"I should go." She reached for her purse. "I don't want to be late for that meeting."

If he would just let it go…

One beat, two, then three passed before he looked away. Her heart stumbled on each one.

"I'll give you a number where I can be contacted. I'll need your number, as well. Call if there's a problem I should know about." He was walking back toward the mudroom as he spoke. "Otherwise, I'll contact you with a rendezvous time and place later this evening."

"Okay." She dug out her cell phone. "What's the number?"

As he provided the necessary digits, she entered them into her phone. Then she gave him her cell number.

"Do you have any idea what time you'll call?" If he took her back to her hotel and all she had was his assurance that he would call, what was to keep him from ditching her? What if something went wrong? Lewis would be seriously ticked off if she let this guy out of her sight and then never heard from him again.

Trust, she reminded herself. She had to trust this man even if logic warned that she shouldn't.

"Go to your meeting," he said. "Then get some sleep." He paused and looked back at her. "You'll need it."

Chapter Thirteen

Phillip Kendall was not a patient man. As the afternoon came and went, he grew more and more restless. He wanted this day to pass, wanted to learn more about this Guardian Angel. He needed to know everything. That was the only way to ensure he paid properly for his grievous sins.

It was true. Phillip paused in his pacing to look out the window that spanned the entire wall. He stared at the view for which he had paid several million dollars. This was his city. His home. His territory. How dare some bastard come into his town and hurt him this way?

He would pay. He would pay so dearly.

"Mr. Kendall?"

Phillip turned to face his personal assistant. "Yes, Owen." Hope fired inside him. "Do you have news?"

Owen was generally very efficient, but this time

Phillip's patience had thinned considerably before getting this update. *If* this was, in fact, an update.

"Nothing yet, sir."

Judging from the pallor on Owen's face it was obvious he had dreaded passing along this information, but he recognized how long he could wait between updates. His time had been up.

"You have a digital image of his face," Phillip argued. "His fingerprints. How could you not have something?"

"Sir." Owen swallowed, the difficulty visible. "It's as if he doesn't exist. He's not in any database—local, state or federal."

"That's impossible."

"I have a contact," Owen said quickly, his posture rigid. "He may be able to help us."

Phillip settled into the luxurious leather chair behind his desk. "What sort of contact?" Was this a ploy for time?

"He's in Homeland Security. If this guy exists outside the shadows of night, I believe my contact might be able to find him."

Phillip considered this strategy. "Perhaps we should take additional precautions tonight."

Owen's expression turned eager. "Shall we detain him tonight?"

No, it was still too soon for that. "We won't take

him into custody just yet," Phillip clarified. "Have our people widen the perimeter. I want someone to track him to wherever he goes after taking custody of the girl."

Owen let his skepticism show. "But if he knows we're following him, he'll attempt to lose us."

Phillip was weary of the conversation. "Let the team leader know that there's a significant bonus if he doesn't lose him and doesn't get caught." Money could make things happen. Owen knew this. Owen's indecisiveness in this matter was becoming quite tedious.

"If he recognizes we're following him and he manages to lose our team," Owen countered, unwilling to let it go, "we may not be able to lure him to the next drop."

That was a risk, yes. But Phillip was out of patience. He needed information on this man. Soon. That way he could plan his strategy for ruining his life—before Phillip ended it entirely.

"See that that doesn't happen," Phillip ordered. "I'm holding you fully responsible for whatever happens tonight."

The pallor was back. Owen nodded. "Yes, sir." Owen turned to go but hesitated. "One other thing, sir."

Phillip resisted the impulse to rant at the man.

Unless he had information—which he did not—there was nothing else to discuss. His assistant should focus on doing his job, not pestering Phillip.

"Savoy called again."

Tension rifled through Phillip. "What does he want now?" Phillip was surrounded by incompetence and greed. He was sick to death of both.

Owen hesitated.

"What?" Phillip demanded.

"He insists that you promised him a bonus if he delivered all six children to you unharmed."

Bonus? "He has the three million," Phillip countered. Greedy son of a bitch. "He doesn't deserve more than that. He should thank me for the opportunity. We did all the legwork." That much was certainly true. Owen had worked day and night choosing just the right children from families that could well afford the ransom.

"Be that as it may," Owen said meekly, "the man was quite adamant about the two-million-dollar bonus he claims you promised him upon delivery of the sixth child."

"Tell him," Phillip offered, "that if he pushes me, I will set the Bureau on his scent. I have many, many contacts, Owen. Savoy should be very afraid of what crossing me could cost him."

Owen nodded stiffly. "I'll pass that along, sir."

Phillip reclined in his chair and watched his assistant hurry away to do his bidding. He would not fail in his tasks. Phillip had known Owen too long to be concerned about whether or not he would succeed. Owen would not sleep again until he was certain Phillip's wishes were carried out.

Phillip smiled. By this time tomorrow he would have the name he sought. Then he would learn all there was to know about this Guardian Angel.

His vengeance would be swift and exact. Before dying, this man would know pain more intimately than he knew himself.

Chapter Fourteen

At three o'clock the Bureau's postmortem regarding the rescue of Kira Robbins was called to order.

The Bureau had nothing.

No name, no face, nothing.

The Guardian Angel was not in any database known to civilized man.

So far they had not made the connection between the park and a two-year-old rescue made by Guardian Angel. Or, if they had, they were keeping that part out of the briefing until the theory could be substantiated.

"You get any sleep this morning?"

Ann had just pushed out of her seat when Frank Lewis approached her.

"Yes, thankfully." That part was partially true. The hour she'd gotten counted, sort of. She hoped like hell he would leave it at that. The last thing she needed was him seeing any deceit in her eyes. She never had been that good at lying.

This was definitely lying. Obstruction of justice and a couple of other unlawful things. The professional risk had been playing heavily on her conscience since she'd returned to her hotel. It annoyed her to no end that she'd had to wear that damned blindfold when she'd left Nathan's home. He had no intention of her discovering his true identity.

She shuddered inwardly as she recalled him asking her about that incident when she was a kid. He'd damn sure done his research on her. She didn't like that he knew so much about her and she knew nothing about him.

"I tried calling your room a couple of times," Lewis said. "Your cell phone's battery must have been spent. I couldn't get through on that, either."

Ann draped her purse handle on her shoulder. "Yeah, it was dead. I forgot to plug it in." Her purse felt inordinately light without the weight of the weapon pulling at her shoulder. She'd left it in her room for this meeting. She hadn't wanted to have to explain how she'd come into possession of it.

"How about you?" She shifted the conversation to him. "Did you get any sleep?"

That was doubtful. Agents got little sleep when embroiled in a high-profile case like this.

Lewis shook his head. "I'll catch up when this is over."

That was what they always said. Catching up on one's sleep when in the employment of the Federal Bureau of Investigations was a pipe dream.

Ann laughed softly. "I've heard that before."

Lewis managed a smile that looked seriously fatigued. "You want to get an early dinner? There's a great Italian place close to your hotel."

His invitation was tempting. She was hungry. She'd barely touched the sandwich Nathan had prepared. But she couldn't be tied up when he called. She glanced at the clock on the wall. Quarter past five. There was plenty of time, most likely, before he called. And she had to eat. Might as well be with Lewis. Maybe he would be less suspicious of her if she went along with his offer.

"That sounds good." She'd have to work at keeping dinner conversation away from the case. Usually she would want to discuss the case they were working on, but not this time. The fewer questions she had to evade, the better off she would be.

The drive to the restaurant was relaxed. The conversation revolved around how Baltimore had changed in the past couple of years and the inevitable changes at the Bureau in response to rising terror threats. Ann thought she was safe for the duration, but once the orders were placed with the waiter, the mood changed with unexpected abruptness.

"Guardian Angel has had no further contact with you?" Lewis sipped his water as he waited for her response as if they had all the time in the world—and as if he hadn't just suggested she'd been contacted.

Well, she had. But he couldn't know that.

Right, wrong or indifferent, she had made a deal.

"That's the sort of thing I would have had to report, don't you think?" She answered his question with a question to prevent having to tell an outright lie and risk his noticing.

He considered her at length, then went on. "You said you would call me if you heard from him."

The statement was as close to an accusation as he dared without any proof. "That's right." She puckered her brow into a frown. "Where are you going with this, Lewis? We've worked together on a lot of cases and I've never felt as if you didn't trust me."

Guilt slid into position on her shoulders and at the same time lined his brow.

He nodded, set his glass aside. "The fact that this guy is like a ghost is getting to me." He turned his glass round and round. "The director has all of us in the hot seat. If we don't bring this guy in soon, there's going to be hell to pay. The mayor, the governor, they're pushing us for results."

"I understand where you're coming from, Lewis," Ann offered. "The Colby Agency is expecting results from me, as well. It's not a pleasant place to be when you don't have squat."

He said something else, but Ann was distracted by her cell phone vibrating in her jacket pocket. She covertly reached into the pocket and removed it. She had a new text message. Careful not to let Lewis see the screen, she checked the message.

Agent Lewis appears to have a thing for you, Ann.

Ann's face flushed and she rubbed at her eye with her left hand to cover the reaction. It took every ounce of willpower she possessed not to look around the restaurant to see if he was there…watching.

The phone vibrated in her hand, warning that there was another text message.

"That looks like us," Lewis said as the waiter approached with a laden tray.

"Great, I'm starved," Ann chimed in, grateful for the distraction.

While the waiter settled the entrées in front of them, she checked her latest message. It gave the meeting place and time. Ten o'clock. Hours away. She should relax. Enjoy the meal. But she couldn't. She kept thinking about the little girl, Sherry Curtis. Would she really be released safe and sound at midnight, the way Kira Robbins had been?

Was Nathan here...watching Ann right now?

She couldn't help herself. She had to look. Allowing her gaze to wander the room, she lingered at each table as long as she dared. No Nathan. But he had to be close. Goose bumps had risen on her flesh, warning her that he wasn't far away.

This was ridiculous. Why did she even care?

When the waiter moved away from their table, Lewis asked, "Do you think we'll see another child released the way Kira Robbins was?"

Ann shifted her gaze from him to her entrée. "We can certainly hope." The idea that she was keeping significant details from Lewis made her feel rotten. But she had to see this through if there was any chance another child actually would be released.

Lewis cut into his medium-rare steak. "I have a copy of those financial transactions from each of the six abductions. I was finally cleared to pass those along to you."

She did meet his eyes this time. "Thanks. That could prove helpful."

If the Bureau hadn't been able to track down the owner of the account to which the funds had been wired, chances were she wouldn't be able to, either. But Lucas Camp, Victoria's husband, had contacts in the CIA as well as Interpol. Interpol had a way of obtaining information the CIA and FBI couldn't seem to get their hands on at times. Although she felt certain Lewis didn't intend for her to share the information, she could trust Lucas. And if he could help, that could hasten the recovery of those children. Maybe it would even save Nathan from whatever the sadistic jerks had planned for him.

She wasn't supposed to care what happened to him...but somehow she just couldn't pretend that she didn't.

He had gotten to her.

Not once in her life had she allowed that to happen.

Too bad the first time had to be now.

11:48 p.m.

THE TIME HAD crawled by so far.

Ann's legs cramped from staying crouched in one position for so long. She didn't dare stand at this point. Any movement could be picked up by night vision, and then the scumbags delivering Sherry Curtis could back out. Could disappear with that little girl. Ann would hold her position for however long it took.

Nathan waited in a location closer to the ancient building's entrance. Like her, he hadn't moved during the past hour and a half.

The idea was to get here early enough to watch the unsubs put the girl into position and maybe get a handle on who was behind this scheme. Ann's respiration and pulse rate hadn't slowed to normal since her arrival on the scene. Nathan had rendezvoused with her at ten. Their interaction had been brief and to the point before moving.

Stationed in a copse of trees some hundred yards away from the old schoolhouse's entrance, she had an excellent view of the street and the untamed landscape. If anyone arrived by vehicle or on foot, she would know it. The building was currently undergoing renovations. In a few months it would reopen as a seniors' center.

Nathan's position was barely a dozen yards from the front entrance, shielded by a dilapidated fence that separated the structure from the too-close intersection. The streets probably hadn't been where they are now when the old school was originally built.

After leaving Lewis and the restaurant, Ann had passed the bank account information to

Victoria. Having a husband who was a former CIA field director was an enviable asset for the Colby Agency. If Lucas could uncover the identity of the account owner, they would have somewhere to start with nailing these bastards. Ann was certain the person or persons delivering the child tonight would not be the perps behind the abductions. These would be hired security professionals. But they could possess important information.

Her hand sought the firm, cool feel of the forty-caliber nestled in her waistband. She had to be prepared for whatever went down tonight. As easy as last night had been, tonight could turn into an all-out war.

Ann's cell phone vibrated. She lifted the phone from her pocket and checked the caller ID display. Her breath stalled in her throat.

Agent Frank Lewis.

Damn.

She couldn't ignore it. He would just send someone to her hotel room or show up there himself. That would be bad considering she wasn't at her hotel.

"Martin." She hated saying her name out loud, but speaking too low was out of the question. That would only make Lewis suspicious.

"Hey, Ann, this is Frank."

She moistened her lips, steadied her breathing. "Hey, Lewis, what's up?"

"We received an anonymous tip that there was going to be another release tonight."

A rumble of shock went through her. "Really?" What the hell was going on here?

Before she could grab on to some logical explanation, he went on. "I thought I'd swing by and pick you up. I'm headed to the location now."

Ann's gaze riveted to the street in front of the old schoolhouse. "Uh…well, I was just getting out of the shower. Why don't you give me the location and I'll meet you there as soon as I'm dressed?"

Not even daring to breathe, Ann listened as he rattled off the address.

A *different* location. Not here. Thank God.

But who would have called with this anonymous tip? Was this some random caller or was the scumbag running this show up to something new?

"Okay, I'll be there," she assured him.

She put her phone away and drew in a shaky gulp of air. Then the idea that the Bureau had gotten a tip about a release tonight sank fully into her brain. What was going on here? Was this the unsub's way of ensuring that the Bureau didn't show up at this location?

She needed to pass this information on to

Nathan. As important as it was to keep out of sight and not make any noise, this intelligence was essential to their ability to make rational decisions.

Rather than make a call, considering just how close he was to the entrance, she opted for text messaging. She passed along what Lewis had told her as quickly and efficiently as possible.

A diversion was his answer.

She agreed.

This unsub intended to cover all bases. He or they had made no mistakes so far and evidently didn't intend to start. Like her, the unsub had probably considered the possibility that the Bureau might see the developing pattern as far as drop locations went and had taken this measure to ensure no interference.

Without the Guardian Angel connection, Ann had to wonder if the Bureau or she would ever have gotten anywhere near the unsub with the lack of evidence they had been able to collect.

An investigator's nightmare, that was what this case amounted to. An unwinnable scenario save for sheer luck or utter coincidence. But then, Ann didn't really believe in either. Somehow there was more behind this than the obvious. The real question was would they ever learn what the other element was?

There was something she couldn't see. Someone or something more than the obvious.

A sound behind her silenced her heart, evacuated the air from her lungs. She didn't move, just listened.

Footsteps coming right at her.

She was dressed in black, with her hair tucked beneath a black skullcap. There was no way anyone could see her hidden the way she was, unless…

They were using thermal technology.

Damn it.

Her fingers tightened around the butt of her weapon at the same instant that the muzzle of another nudged the back of her head.

"Get up."

The gruff male voice left no room for argument.

She raised her hands and slowly rose to her feet.

A swift hand reached around and snatched the Glock from her hand.

"Where's your friend?"

As still as her heart had been moments ago, it now pounded mercilessly against her sternum. "I don't know what you're talking about. I'm here alone."

She hadn't expected the blow. A fist slammed right into the small of her back.

She went down on all fours.

"Where is he?"

Bile rushed into her throat and Ann restrained the need to puke up her dinner. She took several big gulps of air but somehow managed in between to blurt, "I don't know what you're talking about."

A booted foot connected with her abdomen.

This time she lost the contents of her stomach. Her arms and legs shook with the need to curl into a protective ball.

"I'll ask you once more. *Where...is...he?*"

"He's in the SUV," she cried between pants for air. "Down the block."

The cap was yanked off her head and fingers twisted into her hair and hauled her to her feet. "The SUV is empty, *bitch.* Now tell me where he is!"

She got a good look at the guy's masked face. Dark eyes and a big nose. Couldn't make out much else.

"If he's not in the SUV—" she gagged as her stomach roiled some more "—then I don't know where he is. But—" she screamed when he twisted her hair tighter "—he's close. You can count on that." She licked her viciously dry lips. "He's close."

The guy suddenly jerked backward. His fingers released her hair.

Nathan and the bastard who'd assaulted her were rolling on the ground. Ann scrambled for her Glock where it lay a few feet away.

The muffled sound of a weapon discharging snapped her attention back to the struggle.

The masked man clambered to an upright position and ran, stumbling as he went.

Ann grabbed her weapon, started to go after the guy but knew she couldn't without checking on Nathan. He was getting up, staggering with the effort to steady himself. "A weapon discharged. You okay?"

"Yeah…yeah, I'm okay." He made a grunting noise that didn't sound okay at all. "I have to get inside. It's midnight."

"Let me go," she urged, noting his stilted movements. "I can do it."

"Get the SUV." He shoved the keys at her.

She started to argue, but he sprinted in the direction of the old schoolhouse before she could organize a protest. Okay. She inhaled a ragged breath. Maybe he wasn't hurt that badly. Get the vehicle before more trouble showed up. Good idea.

Scanning left and right, she bounded to the SUV parked nearly a block from the location of the drop. She hit the unlock button and swung behind the wheel. Her hands shook as she tried to fit the key into the ignition. Her hands were sweating so badly she could barely hang on to the keys.

She started the engine and reached up to shift into drive, when something on her hand snagged her attention. *What the hell?* She didn't dare turn on the interior light.

Wet, sticky.

She sniffed her hand.

Blood.

Fear snaked around her chest and squeezed.

The weapon discharging echoed in her head.

Nathan had lied to her. He was hit.

Either that or the other guy was and Nathan had gotten blood on him.

The memory of his stiff movements charged into her brain next.

"Damn it."

She shifted into drive and allowed the vehicle to roll forward in the dark without the use of headlights.

If he was hit…if he ran into trouble inside…

She slammed on the brakes in front of the schoolhouse, shoved the gearshift back into Park and reached for her door handle.

The passenger-side door suddenly swung open.

"Go!"

Nathan slumped into the passenger seat, the child in his arms. "Go!" he shouted again.

Ann rammed into Drive and floored the accelerator.

In her rearview mirror she watched three men spill into the street, weapons aimed.

Hell!

She darted left. Cut through two yards to get to the street on the next block.

When she had taken several more side streets and made a number of unexpected turns to put some measurable distance between her and the old schoolhouse, she ordered her heart and respiration to calm. The worst was behind them now. No one was tailing them.

She summoned her voice and asked, "Where are you hit?"

"I'm fine, just drive."

She wanted to laugh but couldn't find the energy. That was just like a man.

"I said where are you hit?"

"Keep driving. We'll drop the little girl off at the nearest E.R."

"And you'll need medical attention." Ann flashed him a look—for all the good it would do with him staring forward. The grim set of his jaw told her he was in pain.

Damn it!

"You know I can't do that," he contended. His voice was low, weak.

"Nathan, you have to—"

"Just drive, Ann. Just drive."

"Fine," she snapped.

She would just drive and he could just… continue bleeding.

Damn it.

Chapter Fifteen

Saturday 12:41 a.m.

Baltimore General was the closest hospital. The one thing Nathan couldn't allow was for her to go into the E.R. and leave the child to summon help for him.

Since taking the little girl inside himself was out of the question, he had to take his chances with another tactic.

As soon as Ann had parked in the lot nearest the E.R. entrance, he said, "Take the child inside. Don't speak to anyone. Don't waste time. I need you back out here as quickly as possible."

"You need help," she tossed back at him. "That's what you need."

She made these statements without looking at him. But her profile gave away her true feelings.

Her lips trembled, then tightened with the inclination to say more, but she didn't. The parking lot lights provided sufficient illumination for him to see that she was worried or terrified or maybe both.

The sooner this was done, the better.

"Take her before she starts to cry again."

Sherry Curtis had cried softly for the first five minutes of the getaway. She had finally stopped and he didn't want her upset again. The best way to ensure that didn't happen was to do this now while she was as calm as could be expected.

Ann climbed out of the vehicle and came around to the passenger door. When she opened it, he did something he knew she wasn't going to like. "Give me the keys."

Her fingers instinctively clenched around the requested item. "You need help."

"Give me the keys," he repeated, the effort of maintaining a level tone monumental.

With a huff of frustration, she relented and dangled the keys at him.

He snatched them from her grasp and said what he hoped would prevent her from doing anything rash. "If you don't come out that door alone in one minute, I'm driving away without you."

Her lips formed a grim line, but she didn't

argue. She lifted Sherry Curtis into her arms and headed for the E.R. entrance.

Nathan slid out of the seat, grunted when his feet hit the pavement. He pushed the door shut and walked around the hood to the other side of the vehicle, then he got in behind the wheel. His knees felt a little weak, but he managed the necessary physical exertion. The bleeding wasn't so bad, but he was pretty sure he would need stitches.

He shoved the key into the ignition, started the engine and punched in the number for Charles. "Meet me at the house in half an hour."

He didn't have to explain the situation. At this hour Charles would suspect trouble and would do whatever necessary to take care of Nathan's needs. The man had many talents.

Just when Nathan had decided Ann's minute was up, the E.R. doors slid open and she walked out. Alone, as he'd requested. She hurried across the parking lot and climbed into the passenger seat. Nathan drove away.

"Her blouse was bloody."

He glanced at Ann. "What?"

"Sherry Curtis…." She drew in an unsteady breath. "Her blouse was bloody. I think a nurse saw me before I could get out the door."

He supposed that was unavoidable, but their

options had been limited. There would be cameras in the E.R. This could come back to haunt Ann Martin far more quickly than he cared to speculate.

Right now he had to focus on driving, on getting home. He couldn't worry about Ann learning the address of his home…his only sanctuary. Though he would likely regret it later.

He'd almost gotten to Annapolis when he recognized he couldn't drive any longer. He had lost the feeling in his arms from gripping the steering wheel so tightly. He couldn't risk going on.

"What're we doing?" she asked as he eased over to the side of the road.

"You should drive from here."

She got out and started around the hood. Rather than get out, he lifted one leg, then the other over the console before hefting himself into the passenger seat.

When she had climbed behind the wheel, then pulled back onto the road, he gave her the necessary instructions for reaching his home just in case he passed out before then.

She didn't question him, just drove. He was thankful for the silence.

He had questions about tonight, but those would just have to wait, as well.

ANN PULLED INTO the driveway of the magnificent house. She had known it would be beautiful, but she couldn't have imagined just how much so. The streetlights, she felt certain, didn't do it justice.

"Nathan." She gently shook his shoulder. He'd been so quiet and still. Trepidation fluttered along her nerve endings during that extended moment when he made no move to respond. When his eyes opened, she relaxed a little and said, "I need the code to your gate."

He muttered the series of numbers and she entered them. The gate slid open, and she took her foot off the brake to allow the SUV to roll through. Once she was beyond the gate, it closed once more. The garage door opened, so she parked inside. As she exited the vehicle she caught just a quick glance of the moonlight shimmering against the water across the narrow street that ran in front of his home. Then the garage door closed. Another black SUV was parked in the garage. She wondered just how many black SUVs the man had access to.

Nathan's movements were slow and stiff. A man met them in the mudroom. That he looked so concerned for Nathan alleviated the apprehension his sudden appearance sparked. Evidently Nathan had called while she'd been taking Sherry Curtis into the hospital and requested that this man meet them here.

"Let's get to the clinic and get this taken care of, Mr. Tyler."

Tyler. Okay, so now she knew his last name. Or at least the one he used.

Clinic? Nathan had a clinic in his house? Was this man a doctor or nurse?

Nathan thanked the man and allowed him to lead the way beyond the kitchen and down a side corridor. Ann followed. When the two men paused in front of a door, the stranger said to her, "Perhaps you should wait in the parlor, ma'am."

When she didn't readily agree, Nathan met her gaze. "I would appreciate your continued cooperation."

She nodded but didn't move until the two had disappeared behind the door.

Ann felt weak with relief—or something on that order—once the idea that Nathan's situation was being attended to penetrated the cloud of slowly dissipating anxiety cloaking her ability to reason.

At least now she knew where he lived, knew his last name. Nathan Tyler of Annapolis.

She crossed her arms over her chest and moved down the main hall. There was no reason she couldn't explore the house while she waited. No point standing around.

A parlor, a den, a study. All richly appointed. All warm and inviting. The man had good taste in decorating, she'd give him that.

The enormous kitchen was like something out of *Architectural Digest*. Despite the exquisite details, however, it somehow fit with the age and historic presence of the house. A very difficult balance to achieve, if she had her guess.

Okay, enough with the trip into the *House & Garden* zone. She ran her fingers through her hair. The dried blood smear on her hand reminded her of what was taking place behind that door on the other side of the house.

Nathan needed professional medical attention, not some amateur patch job.

After a couple of wrong turns, she found a powder room. She washed her hands twice, then a third time just to get the smell off. Then she washed her face and tidied her hair. There was blood on her blouse, but not that much.

What she really needed was a shower and a change of clothes.

She wandered back to the kitchen for a drink. Her mouth and throat were terribly dry. A bottle of water from the fridge did the trick. Her stomach rumbled when she noticed the bowl of freshly prepared salad. She licked her lips. As hungry as she suddenly realized she was, she would wait for an invitation.

Twenty minutes had passed since they'd arrived back at the house. She decided to wander back toward the room where Nathan was receiving whatever treatment the stranger was able to give him. Who knew—maybe the man was a doctor or a paramedic. A friend of Nathan's, certainly.

Nathan Tyler.

Who was Nathan Tyler?

Since the door to the clinic was still closed, she turned and made her way to the office he'd taken her into before. The one with all the monitors. Just like before, several of the monitors were set to news channels while others displayed screen savers. None of the local news channels were showing anything about the discovery of Sherry Curtis in the E.R. But it wouldn't be long.

Ann walked around the room. There really was nothing to look at. No awards or diplomas gracing the walls. No stacks of papers on the desk. Clean, neat. The blinds were drawn tight, as they were elsewhere in the house. There wasn't a single clue to the identity of her host.

Who was Nathan Tyler?

That was the question of the hour.

A man of means, certainly. A man who would risk his own life to help a child, definitely.

But who was he?

What was it about his past that made him feel such a strong connection to her? Allowed him to recognize the pain she had suffered as a child during that twenty-four hours she had been lost? A twenty-four-hour period that no one knew the truth about. Not another living soul. She'd kept it that way for more than fifteen years. She wasn't about to change her strategy now…not even if it helped her learn exactly who Nathan Tyler was.

"Ms. Martin?"

Ann's breath caught. She turned sharply to face the man who had spoken her name.

Him. The stranger who'd hustled Nathan into that room he called the clinic.

"How is he?" That was the right question to ask, though she wanted to know who this man was and what credentials he had that permitted him to care for a gunshot wound. None of that was particularly relevant at the moment.

"The wound was not as bad as the amount of blood Mr. Tyler lost made it appear," he explained. "Clean entrance and exit wounds in soft tissue only. Left side just above the hip. He'll need some rest to recover from the initial trauma, but I'm sure he'll be up and around by midmorning. I've left him an antibiotic and I'll redress the wounds later today."

He was right. It was today, not tonight. Two-forty. God, she was tired.

"Can I see him?"

"Yes, of course." He glanced at her. "By the way, I'm Charles. This way, please."

She followed Charles back into the main hall and then along that more narrow side corridor. That was when she decided she needed a few answers. Pretending those answers didn't matter was just more than she could continue to endure.

"Are you a physician?"

He chuckled. "Not anymore."

What exactly did that mean?

As if she'd asked the question aloud, he went on. "I was accused of negligent homicide a few years back, and that ended my medical career. For a while I lived in a bottle to nurse my depression. But Mr. Tyler found me and now I take care of him."

Negligent homicide? "That's…too bad."

He paused at the door to the room where he'd treated Nathan. "Actually, it was a blessing in disguise. I have a great deal more time with my family, and for the first time in my life I'm not hypertensive." Charles gazed at the door as if he could see through it. "He gave me my life back."

Now that was looking at the bright side of a bad situation. Looked as if Nathan Tyler was a rescuer of more than small children.

The word *hero* echoed through her mind.

She pushed the concept away. Keeping some sense of distance here was necessary. She hadn't exactly done a stellar job so far. There would be consequences for her actions the past few hours. Professional and personal.

Charles rapped on the door before opening it. "Mr. Tyler?"

Nathan was propped against what appeared to be an examination table. Ann glanced briefly around the room, some part of her brain recognizing that it was, indeed, a clinic. But before her mind could loiter on the idea for long, her attention fixated once more on the man. Though tall and lean, his frame was well-muscled. If she'd had any questions before, she now knew for certain since his shirt was history.

"Charles, before you go," Nathan said, "would you see that Ms. Martin has something to eat? It's been a long night and I'm sure she's weary and hungry."

She was too preoccupied with inventorying

Nathan's physical assets to care. His damaged shirt lay on the floor. His jeans hung low on his hips. His sculpted torso made her think of one of those ads for a popular clothing store. The guy was definitely in shape. All those acres of sleek skin were marred only by the white bandage on his left side.

"You okay?" she asked. The question was pretty much redundant since she could clearly see that he was fine, but she'd had to ask.

"I'm fine," he assured her.

This was the first time she'd seen his hair loose about his shoulders. She had thought she wouldn't like it so long, but she'd been wrong. The urge to touch it was nearly overpowering.

"Why don't we move to the kitchen," Charles offered, "and prepare you a proper dinner."

"That's really not necessary," she protested. "A shower and clean clothes are at the top of my list right now."

"And you, Mr. Tyler?" Charles asked.

"I think that goes for me, as well," Nathan agreed.

"Very well. If there's nothing else I can do…"

Charles said good-night and then took his leave.

"I'll show you to a guest room."

Ann's attention swung from the departing Charles to her host. He'd crossed the room and now stood next to her. She really must be tired not to have picked up on the fact that he'd moved.

Nathan preceded her up the stairs. She wondered how he still had the stamina to endure what was no doubt a painful, tiring journey. Her attention got caught up in mapping the unexpected details of his back—it was a stark contrast to the sleek, smooth skin of his chest and abdomen.

Her mouth went as dry as dirt as she realized what each obviously old scar signified. Nathan Tyler had been beaten repeatedly and over an extended period of time.

Ann nearly stumbled as she reached the second-story landing. Who had done this to him?

Midway down the upstairs corridor he paused at an open door. "I think you'll find everything you need. If not, I'm at the end of the hall. Good night."

"Good night," she called after him since he didn't glance back or wait around for her response. He was exhausted, she felt certain. He needed rest more than she did considering what he'd been through.

Her mind conjured the image of all those scars. Some were faded to nearly nothing, others were still ugly despite the passage of time.

At some point she would ask him for the story

behind those scars. If he'd wanted to hide them from her, he certainly hadn't done a very good job. Maybe he wanted her to ask.

Enough. She was too tired to analyze anything else tonight. She went into the room he'd assigned her and took a look around.

The room was enormous and, of course, exquisitely decorated. She passed through to the en suite bath, stripped off her clothes and climbed into the shower. Her abdomen and back were bruised from the beating she had taken. Breathing wasn't painful, but it wasn't exactly comfortable. She was reasonably sure she didn't have any cracked ribs. She'd had one once, and they hurt like the dickens. This was not that kind of pain.

When she stepped out of the shower, she grabbed the fluffy white robe from the back of the door. This would do until she had clean clothes. Maybe if she took her clothes downstairs, she could locate a washer and dryer.

She gathered her discarded clothes and her stomach rumbled loudly. Might as well do something about that while she searched for the laundry room.

The basement had been a storeroom with everything *but* a washer and dryer, she remembered. No point going down there. There had been a door in the mudroom that didn't lead into the garage. Maybe that was it. She went there first. Sure enough, the door led into a spacious laundry room. She tossed her clothes into the washer and set the cycle. After she ate, she would check to see if things were ready to go into the dryer.

As she entered the kitchen, movement stopped her cold, but then she realized it was only Nathan. Clad in pajama bottoms and still shirtless, he was considering the options in the fridge. She took the time to study the way the flannel pants clung so precariously low on his hips. The slightest wrong move could send them plunging to the floor. That would be no hardship, if what she'd seen so far was any indication of his physique.

"You decided you were hungry after all," he said when he looked up and discovered her watching him.

"I saw the salad earlier." She moved closer, gestured to the covered bowl on the middle shelf. "I've been thinking about it ever since."

"Salad it will be, then." He placed the bowl on the counter next to the fridge.

"You—" she took hold of his arm and guided him to a stool "—need to sit. I'll take care of this." His skin felt warm against her fingers, sent a tiny pang of desire whirling through her.

He didn't argue with her suggestion.

"So, Nathan Tyler," she said as she prepared his plate, then her own, "is that your real name?"

"That's what Charles called me, isn't it?"

As if that answered the question. "I have a feeling people call you what you want them to call you."

"Nathan Tyler is who I am now."

Aha. She'd been right. "Who were you before?"

"I don't think you want me to answer that question."

Maybe she didn't. If he told her the truth about his past, she would be obliged to tell him her own—and she didn't talk about that to anyone. Not her family or her friends and certainly not to a man who was both a stranger and a possible enemy. Though she hadn't treated him like an enemy in any shape or form.

She had a very bad feeling that her actions were going to come back to haunt her in a very big way…very soon.

"Dressing?" She looked at him expectantly.

"Italian."

She decided on the same. As she drizzled her salad, she asked, "Do you think the third child will be released after what happened this time?"

He speared a cherry tomato. "It depends upon whether or not wounding me was the only intent.

If whoever is behind these abductions wants me dead, then he's not finished yet."

That was the part that bothered her the most. If he wanted Nathan dead, why not kill him? He'd had ample opportunity, especially if he had gone the sniper route. The seemingly ill-planned, bumbling tactics of what were clearly professionals just didn't fit.

"Are you all right?"

The look of concern he pointed in her direction made her feel self-conscious about her lack of clothing beneath the fluffy bathrobe. It also jerked her back to the here and now.

"I have some bruises but nothing that won't fade in a few days."

She couldn't remember the last time she'd had the crap kicked out of her like that. Her stomach roiled even now as she thought of the kick in the gut she'd taken from that scumbag.

"Perhaps I should do this alone next time." He tucked a cucumber slice into his mouth and chewed with purpose. "Assuming there is a next time."

"I went out on a limb for you," she argued, not about to be left out at this point. "No way are you leaving me out of the loop now." She didn't bother going into what would happen when Lewis learned what she'd done instead of meeting him. She'd probably be arrested.

Nathan knew there were things he needed to say to her. Like the apology lodged in his throat regarding his inability to protect her. He should have stayed closer to her. He had allowed her to be hurt, and that was unacceptable. She was already doing far more for him than she should. Her life and her career were on the line because of him.

Then there was the nagging fact that she now knew his name. He hoped that wouldn't become a problem, but he had to anticipate that possibility.

"I should have protected you tonight," he said, the words sounding far too impotent for his liking. "I should have been better prepared."

"You aren't to blame for what happened to me," she countered. "I should've heard him coming way before he was on top of me. That was my mistake."

They ate in silence from there. By the time they finished, he could see the mounting fatigue in the set of her delicate shoulders.

"We should turn in," he urged as he placed his plate in the sink.

She settled her plate on top of his. "You're not curious about what the media will report about you this time?"

He'd stopped caring what the media did years ago. The energy was wasted. He had no control over what those vultures did. To think otherwise was a mistake.

"No." He ushered her toward the hall. "I've learned to ignore what they report. Most of the time it's as far from the truth as can be gotten."

They climbed the stairs without speaking, a testament to their growing fatigue. She appeared to be fading fast.

Or so he'd thought until she stopped at her door and faced him.

"How long has Charles worked for you?"

She never tired of attempting to trip him up.

"I've known Charles for many years. When he was falsely accused of negligent homicide and found guilty, I offered him an opportunity to rebuild his life." *And it worked,* he didn't add.

"He certainly has immense respect for you."

"The admiration is mutual," Nathan admitted.

"Did you take the antibiotic he gave you?"

Nathan nodded. "He made sure of that."

"How soon do you think we'll hear any news?"

By *news* he understood that she meant orders from the man still holding four of the six children.

"I don't know. Last time it was only a few hours. This time—" he shrugged "—who knows?"

Standing in the doorway to the guest room, she searched his eyes again in that probing way that made him want to squirm.

"Good night, Nathan Tyler."

"Good night."

This time she closed the door. He stood there a moment, gathering his thoughts, then moved on to the end of the hall and his own suite of rooms.

Time to sleep.

He would need all his strength, all his powers of strategizing to go up against his enemy. He was certain, absolutely certain that this was far from over.

All he had to do was keep the Bureau at bay until he'd nailed this bastard. Not an easy feat.

But he would damn sure try his best.

He would need her help again.

Whoever this enemy was, his time was running out very fast.

Faster than he knew.

Chapter Sixteen

"This is your failure!" Owen repeated the words Mr. Kendall had hurled at him.

Owen was sick, sick, sick of taking the blame for everything.

It wasn't his fault the miscommunication had caused the security detail to lose the Guardian Angel. One member had jumped the gun, attempted to take down the woman.

At least now the woman's identity had been confirmed.

Ann Martin.

Former FBI advisor and now an investigator for the Colby Agency out of Chicago. Katherine Fowler had hired her to find her daughter.

Ann Martin knew who the Guardian Angel was. She was working with him. Getting that information out of Ms. Martin shouldn't be that difficult. All they had to do was catch her alone. Owen suspected that had been the intent of the fool who'd acted out of turn. His lack of foresight had bungled the entire operation.

How had half a dozen professionals lost one black SUV carrying a wounded man, a woman and a child?

The incompetence wasn't Owen's, by God.

It was the low-life mercenaries Mr. Kendall insisted on hiring. Alcoholics and drug addicts. It was a miracle they accomplished anything at all.

Mr. Kendall had been furious when he'd learned that the Guardian Angel had been injured.

"If he dies," Kendall had said, "someone will pay dearly."

Owen knew that someone was him. He was always the one who took the blame for everything.

He was sick of it. Sick, sick, sick.

Now Mr. Kendall wanted the Grider boy. Five-year-old Jeremy Grider. He was to be released at nine this evening. No more midnight rendezvous, Mr. Kendall had insisted.

Nine o'clock in a public place.

This time he was planting a tracking device on the child. For all the good it would do. Guardian Angel always dropped the children off at their homes, if feasible, or at the nearest hospital or around-the-clock medical clinic. The tracking device was just another stupid idea. If Kendall wanted this Guardian Angel, why didn't he just make him trade himself for the release of the other children?

That would be the simplest way to get what he wanted. Uncomplicated. Straightforward.

But no. Kendall didn't work that way. He had some sort of warped sense of justice and gaming strategy. He wanted to learn more about Guardian Angel. Find out his weaknesses and what he cared about so Kendall could make his vengeance all the more brutal.

If he didn't get caught playing these stupid games.

If he didn't get Owen killed.

Owen parked in front of the warehouse. The remaining four children and two caretakers were here. Owen was to instruct the caretakers personally on where to deliver the Grider boy this evening. There would be no mistakes this time, Kendall had reiterated. One caretaker would deliver the boy, the other would stay with the three remaining children. Owen was to deliver the tracking device and these instructions. Personally. Now.

No mistakes.

Or someone would pay. Dearly.

Owen walked to the warehouse entrance, conscious of the hustle and bustle at the other ends of the block. It was broad daylight, just past noon, and he was doing this crap. What if someone saw him? What if the connection between the children and this warehouse were made at some point in the investigation? Someone might remember that Owen had been here.

Kendall didn't care about protecting anyone but himself. Well, Owen had news for him: if he went down, Kendall was going down, too.

Owen entered the code and waited for the lock to release on the massive entry door. When the release sounded, he went inside and headed for the innermost room, where the children were being held.

Two things assaulted his senses five feet inside the warehouse.

The sharp metallic smell of blood.

And the total absence of sound.

No DVD cartoon noises. No murmur of voices. Nothing.

The hair on the back of Owen's neck stood on end as he continued toward the door to the room where the children should be.

Outside that door, sprawled at an odd angle, was one of the caretakers.

The bullet holes in his chest had leaked what

appeared to be the better part of the life-giving blood from his body. Owen didn't need to check; this guy was most assuredly dead.

The door to the room was ajar. Owen listened for several seconds, heard nothing but silence, then pushed his way inside since the door seemed to be blocked.

The blockage he encountered was the second caretaker's body splayed on the floor.

The room was deserted.

The children were gone.

Owen turned all the way around in the room, his heart pounding harder with each passing second.

This couldn't be.

The children were gone.

His cell phone vibrated in his pocket and Owen shrieked. The phone. Just the phone. He dug it out and glared at the display.

Mr. Kendall.

Oh, God.

What did he do? What did he tell him?

The phone vibrated again, insistently.

Owen pressed the necessary button. "Yes." He swallowed to dampen his dry throat.

"There's been a change in plan."

Owen wasn't sure how to respond. Did he tell

him the children were missing…or did he simply listen?

He opted for the latter.

"Your contact at Homeland Security finally came through. I know who he is." Laughter echoed across the airwaves. "I even know where he lives."

"That's excellent, Mr. Kendall." If they were able to get this guy without the children, then perhaps the fact they were missing wouldn't matter so much.

"Let's abort your previous orders for now. Return to the office. We're going to go about this an entirely different way."

"Yes, sir."

Owen ended the call and gulped in a badly needed lungful of air.

Thank God.

He might just live through this.

He stared at the man on the floor.

Too bad for those children.

Chapter Seventeen

Ann awoke to her cell phone vibrating on the bedside table.

She blinked, tried to think where she was.

Nathan Tyler's home.

She sprang upright in bed.

What time was it?

She grabbed her cell and checked the time. One-oh-five.

Damn!

The words *Missed Call* appeared on the screen. She checked the number and her heart bumped against her sternum.

Lewis.

He'd called six times. She turned off her phone as the realization that they could track her location using that connection settled deep into her gut.

Ignoring his call was out of the question. But she couldn't call from here.

Throwing back the cover, she dropped her feet to the floor and hurried to the bathroom to take care of business. Her gut clenched as her abdominal and back muscles tightened. She was as sore as hell from the beating she'd taken.

When she had washed her face and combed her hair, she would go in search of her clothes. She had put them in the washer before going into the kitchen in search of food.

As she moved from the bathroom back into the bedroom, she drew up short when she found her clothes folded neatly on the dresser. Her face flushed at the idea that someone had even folded her panties. She dressed quickly. How had she slept so long? She should have been up hours ago.

The smell of fresh-brewed coffee greeted her on the first floor. She followed the aroma to the kitchen. She poured herself a cup and went in search of her host. As she suspected, she found him in his office. Each of the monitors broadcasting a local news channel was reporting on the release of Sherry Curtis.

Nathan glanced up at her as she entered the room. "Good afternoon."

"Afternoon." She started to ask why he'd let

her sleep so long, but the question was pointless. It was done now. There was no taking back the time she had lost.

"The reporters are suggesting that the person who dropped the little girl at the E.R. was caught on surveillance tapes, but no footage or confirmation has been released as of yet."

No wonder Lewis was trying to get in touch with her. Not only had she stood him up, he now likely knew why. Man, she was in serious trouble here. And yet she couldn't dredge up any remorse. Two of those six children were back home with their parents. How could she regret that?

"Lewis tried to call me," she informed Nathan. Might as well get that out in the open, too. Lewis would have people looking for her already. "I turned off my cell so they couldn't use it to track my location."

"They can't track you here," Nathan explained. "I have a jamming device. They can only get as close as the nearest cell tower."

That was good to know. She needed to keep that line open. If Victoria attempted to get in touch with her with news from Lucas's search on the bank account and routing number, Ann needed to be available. She turned her cell back on since there was no worry about tracking.

She sipped her coffee, relished the rich, warm flavor as she watched last night's events reported over and over on the various stations. The release of Sherry Curtis was the big news.

A tad of regret trickled through her at the idea that she not only needed to call Lewis but she needed to touch base with Katherine Fowler, as well. Katherine would be beside herself with both anticipation and trepidation. She deserved an update.

Two children had been returned so far, but last night things had not gone so well. Anything could happen at this point. And it could just as easily be bad as it could be good.

"I need to check in with my office and touch base with Lewis."

Nathan's attention settled on her. "You know he's going to want you to come in. There could be criminal charges levied if you refuse."

She nodded. "I'm aware of that possibility."

Nathan set aside the papers he was reviewing. "You could always tell him that I coerced you. He can't prove otherwise."

Ann scoffed. "Like he'd believe that. Lewis knows me too well to believe anyone could force me to do anything I didn't want to unless they were holding a gun to my head. And even then I might refuse."

Nathan started to say something else, but a chime from his computer drew his attention.

"I have an invitation," he said, his voice uncharacteristically serious.

"Is he going to release another child?" Hope surged, and Ann said a quick prayer that just maybe that was the case. Four children to go. They needed all of them home safe and sound.

His silence as he continued to read from the screen had her gut twisting into knots.

"Apparently he's going to release all the children at nine tonight."

Ann knew a moment of exhilaration, but that passed abruptly. "What's the price?" There would be a price. This scumbag hadn't been playing this game all this time to suddenly throw his hands up and walk away.

Nathan met her gaze. "Me."

For whatever reasons, the unsub had lured Nathan to two different locations to pick up a missing child. Each time he had walked away with the child. Now, out of the blue, the rules were being changed.

Something was wrong.

"This doesn't feel right." Her nerves jangled at the idea that this was some kind of trap where there would be no upside.

"That may be," he allowed, "but I can't risk ignoring the offer. If there's any chance he'll release the children, I have to agree to his terms."

All this time she'd been toying with the concept that this guy was the real thing—an actual hero. And now she knew for sure.

He was definitely textbook hero material.

She glanced at the time on her cell. "We have several hours. Let me call in backup from my people at the Colby Agency. This doesn't have to be a sacrifice. We just have to outmaneuver this guy."

The idea made sense. The investigators at the Colby Agency were the cream of the crop. The best in the business. They could get this done. All she needed was his cooperation. The agency jet could have backup here in a couple of hours.

"I have specific instructions to come alone," he countered. "That's what I have to do."

She couldn't let him do that.

"There's no guarantee he'll release the children even after you've turned yourself over to him. You need an alternate plan."

Nathan pushed out of his chair. "I'll take your suggestion under advisement on one condition."

Her guard went up. "What condition is that?"

He came around to her side of the desk and

propped his hip on the edge. "Tell me what happened in those woods when you were nine."

"This isn't the time," she protested.

He looked her dead in the eye and said, "This could be the only time."

The trail of scars that told the tale of his own past barged unbidden into her thoughts. "All right. I'll tell you." Even as the words left her mouth, she had second thoughts. Her heart thumped hard as she added, "*If* you'll tell me about the scars."

His expression changed instantly. His own guard locked into place and the line of his jaw hardened.

An impasse.

"It's a fair deal," she offered, determined not to back off now. If she could share that night with him, he could damn sure share his secrets with her.

Those piercing blue eyes looked straight into her soul, making it hard to breathe…impossible to think.

The intensity there abruptly withdrew. The change left her struggling for balance. His entire demeanor grew distant, untouchable.

"My name was Nolan Thompson. I grew up outside Richmond. I was an only child. My father was an evil bastard who would do anything for money."

Ann could see where this was going. "He left his mark?"

For one second, one fleeting instant, an old hatred glinted in Nathan's eyes.

"Yes." He looked away as if he feared she would see more than he wanted to share. "He liked showing my mother and me who was boss. He particularly liked hurting me."

She ached for him. How could a father do that to his own child? "How old were you before you were able to get away from him?" He had escaped that ugly cycle. She was certain of that.

"When I was eleven, I discovered one of my father's latest moneymaking schemes in the basement."

Ann felt cold. She hugged her arms around herself and braced for the worst.

"He had kidnapped a little girl and was going to deliver her to a man who loved little girls." His jaw tightened with disgust. "I tried to help her escape, but he caught me and beat me unconscious. When I woke up, she was gone and he was drunk."

Dear God. "Were you able to go to the police?"

"Oh, yeah." He closed his eyes a moment before he continued. "In his drunken stupor he decided I needed another beating. I decided I'd had enough. So this time I fought back."

Ann waited through the silence…waited for the other shoe to drop.

"I killed him. My mother insisted to the police that I was making up the story about the little girl."

Just when Ann had reasoned that things could have been worse, she learned that they had been. "Did she tell them that he was hurting you and that you were only defending yourself?"

He shook his head and laughed. "No. She told them she knew nothing about the bruises and scars."

Tears blurred Ann's vision. "What happened?"

"I spent one year in an institution for the mentally unstable and then I stayed in a center for violent juvenile offenders until I was eighteen."

She could easily imagine what he'd suffered during those long years. Even the best facilities weren't that great. "When you were released, did you go home?"

"My mother was dead. There was no one or nothing for me to go back to. So I went to work for a con artist who had a thing for technology." Nathan straightened away from the desk. "I learned I had a knack for creating computer programs, particularly games. That led me to cybersecurity. Eventually I changed my name and became a different person. I left the past behind."

"Wow." No family. No history to look back upon fondly. No old friends. Her gaze met his.

"That's why you don't let anyone close. You don't want anyone to know who you really are." His guard was back up. It wasn't necessary for him to respond to her assessment; she knew she was right. A part of that abused little boy still lived deep inside him and he didn't want anyone to know. He didn't want anyone close.

"Your turn," he said, turning the tables on her.

All the anticipation she'd experienced upon discovering his past vanished, left her cold again. "My past isn't nearly so horrific as yours." It was a delay tactic, pure and simple.

"This isn't a contest, Ann."

Did he have to stand so close? She liked it better when he was leaning against the desk. She backed up a step to put some space between them.

He angled his head in challenge. "You didn't just get lost, did you?"

How could he know that?

"I…" She swallowed at the swelling in her throat. After all these years she should be able to talk about that day…that night…without growing so emotional. It was over, couldn't hurt her anymore. "I was playing in the woods. Like I always did."

She wished he wouldn't look at her that way, as if he needed to analyze each syllable, each movement of her lips.

"Only there was someone else there...watching me."

"Someone you knew?" he guessed.

Her heart skipped a beat. "Yes. He..." She moistened her lips. "He called out to me, said he had something to show me."

The images played out in her mind, making her gut clench and her eyes burn with the emotions crowding into her chest.

"I put my hand in his and skipped along beside him as he led the way." For a moment she got caught up in the memories. She had to remind herself not to look back, to focus, to go on. "We walked for so long. I got tired and complained, but he kept telling me we were almost there."

The darkness closed in on her thoughts. That place. The cave. Dank and smelly. She would never forget the way it smelled...the damp, creepy way the ground had felt beneath her.

"It was a cave," she squeezed out around the constriction in her throat. "He had a flashlight and a sleeping bag in there. Some food and booze." Even now, her stomach heaved at the remembered smell of sour-mash whiskey.

"He raped you."

The three words were uttered so softly, so painfully, that she barely heard them. "Yes."

She swiped at the damned tears sliding down her cheeks. "He said he'd been watching me for a long time and he knew just what I needed. He told me if I ever told anyone, something bad would happen. Then he did it again." Her teeth gritted together to fight the emotions churning like a hurricane. "Eventually he passed out from the whiskey and I ran away."

"They found you the next day," Nathan offered. "And you kept quiet."

She nodded. "He didn't come around much after that. I think maybe he was afraid I might break down and tell someone."

"Is he still alive?"

She laughed to herself. "That's the truly sick part about the whole thing." She nodded. "Yes. He's still alive. Living right where he's always lived. A proud grandfather and occasional poker-playing buddy of my father's."

"You don't go home often because of him, do you?"

She moved her head slowly from side to side. "Nope." She drew in a big breath. "I'm too ashamed of what I let him get away with." She met that piercing gaze with a determined one of her own. "But it was easier to pretend it didn't happen than to face the reality of…it."

He reached out, pulled her into his arms. "It's always easier to pretend," he murmured. "He can't hurt you now—just like my old man can't hurt me."

Except his father was dead. Her silence had allowed a rapist, a pedophile, to live. To get away with it. What the hell was she doing pretending to be a defender of others' rights when she didn't even have the courage to defend her own?

Just like always, she kept the troubling thoughts to herself. Let herself be held by this man who understood better than anyone just how she felt. She pushed her hands under his shirt, allowed her palms and fingers to stroke those scars. They had both been to hell and back and somehow they had survived.

That was something.

His hands moved up to cup her face as he drew away a few inches. "I'm sorry I didn't have the chance to know you before."

He was going to turn himself over to this scumbag.

"There's always tomorrow," she argued. "All we have to do is get through today."

He smiled, and when he did, her heart melted a little.

"When's the last time anyone kissed you, Ann Martin?"

Why did he have to go and ask such a hard question? She shrugged. "Too long ago to remember," she confessed. "In case you haven't noticed, I have intimacy issues."

"Maybe I have time to take care of that."

He kissed her. Lightly, softly. The faintest brushing of his lips against hers.

She leaned into his strong body, hugged him as close as possible. It felt good to be near him… made her body come alive in ways she hadn't allowed herself to feel in years.

He deepened the kiss, still keeping his lips closed. No intrusion, no pushiness. Just a simple, uncomplicated kiss.

Slowly, surely, her body responded, heated to the point where just having his lips touch hers wasn't nearly enough. She wanted—needed—more.

Ann opened for him, let him take it from there. His tongue swept into her mouth, tempting her control. She shivered, held on to him more tightly. She teased his lips with her tongue, not daring to delve inside just yet.

And then he took complete charge. He kissed her the way a man should kiss a woman. With passion and finesse.

Her cell phone vibrated, made her jump.

She pulled away from Nathan. "Sorry."

What was she doing here? It wasn't that she regretted the kiss…or even the conversation. She didn't. But there were more pressing issues to resolve. Four missing children, including the one she had been commissioned to find.

The caller ID on her phone showed a missed call from Victoria Colby-Camp.

"I really have to return this call." She resisted the urge to brush her mouth with the back of her hand. Her lips still burned from his powerful kisses, from his incredible taste.

He nodded his understanding, then walked out of the room, giving her some privacy.

Ann took a moment to pull herself together. She had to get back on track, had to do this right. Katherine Fowler was counting on her.

When she felt rational and calm enough, she made the call. Mildred, Victoria's personal assistant, patched her through to the boss.

"Good afternoon, Victoria, this is Ann. Do you have an update for me?"

"I received a call from Agent Lewis," Victoria said first. "Do I have reason to be concerned?"

Ann cringed. "I've been avoiding his calls," she admitted. "I'm working on a lead I'm not so sure he would be happy about."

"I understand."

Ann blinked. Had she heard right? Of course she had. This was Victoria Colby-Camp. She always backed up her troops. "I believe I'm getting very close," she went on, hoping her boss would understand her need to stay under the Bureau's radar for now.

"I trust your judgment completely," Victoria assured her. "I wouldn't have called, but I have an update from Lucas on those routing and account numbers you provided."

"Great." Ann scrounged up a pen and notepad from Nathan's desk. "I'm ready to copy whatever you have."

"The account is owned by a man who is on a dozen Interpol watch lists. He's a private contractor named Damon Savoy."

"Private contractor? Does he have a specialty?" This sounded like their man. If he was good enough to have made that much of a stir with Interpol, then he could damn sure pull off half a dozen child abductions.

"Hostage retrieval."

If Victoria had said most anything else, Ann would not have been surprised. "Looks like he turned his specialty around and used his skills for taking hostages rather than retrieving them."

"Evidently so. Be very careful, Ann. This man is dangerous. Both Ian and Simon believe you should have backup for this one."

Ian Michaels and Simon Ruhl were Victoria's right-hand men, her seconds in command.

"Let me get back to you on that, Victoria." Ann would have to convince Nathan first. "But I'd appreciate it if preparations could be made so that if I need backup, it can be delivered in a timely manner."

"Done."

Ann discussed a few more details with Victoria before ending the call.

Now all she had to do was convince Nathan to trust her and the Colby Agency.

Considering his background, that might just be asking the impossible.

NATHAN RAN THE name Damon Savoy through every database available to him. He found zip. There was no connection between Savoy and Nathan, past or present. Nor was there a traceable link with any of the kidnap victims that he could find. Other than perhaps Trey Fowler. Fowler worked with Homeland Security. Politically, he'd made his share of enemies. But not a single connection to Savoy showed up in any of the background searches Nathan had performed.

No one was better at digging up dirt on people; Nathan was an expert at finding things others couldn't.

Then again, Savoy made his fortune by contracting out his services. Following that theory, Savoy may have been nothing more than the hired help.

Even with the Savoy name and the verification that he owned the account into which the ransom funds had been wired, ultimately he might not be the man they were looking for.

Ann entered Nathan's office, and his breath left him before he could stop the reaction. There was so much about her to appreciate. Her beauty, her determination and simply the way she moved. He'd never met a woman like her. The truth was he'd never met a woman who made him want a relationship the way she did.

"I spoke with Lewis," she announced. If her subdued posture was any indication, the conversation hadn't gone well.

Nathan reclined in his chair. "I'll bet that was pleasant." The man wanted to take Nathan down something fierce. Lewis had a job to do, and Ann was preventing him from accomplishing that goal.

She lowered into one of the chairs in front of his desk. "He took it better than I expected."

Her fingers traced her brow. Nathan wondered if she had a headache.

"Do you need something for that?"

Startled by the question, she stared at him a moment. "I'm sorry, what was the question?"

And she wanted to help him tonight. She was exhausted. If they were going to survive tonight, he needed total focus. No distractions. No weakness. As helpful as she had been so far, she posed a risk for him. He would not be able to focus fully if she were near. He would be too concerned with keeping her safe. Tonight had to be about securing the release of the other children.

"Do you need something for a headache?"

"No, thank you. I'm fine...."

I'm fine. How many times had the two of them made that statement in the past couple of days? She wasn't fine. He wasn't fine. They were two damaged people trying to be whole, trying to save others from the pain they had endured as children.

A pretty damned unlikely pair of heroes.

He had to get his mind back on the matter at hand. Distraction was his enemy. "What did Lewis say?" *Besides the order to bring me in,* Nathan surmised, but he kept that sidebar to himself.

"I told him what Victoria had discovered about Savoy. She's sending him the complete file. He's going to see what he can find on the guy. If he can find something useful in the next hour, we might be able to use the information to our benefit."

If being the key word there.

"I'm also going to ask Victoria—my boss—to have Ian Michaels and Simon Ruhl standing by in Baltimore if we need their assistance. I hope you're okay with that. You can trust them."

He could argue with her, but he doubted it would do any good. She was worried. For that matter, he was worried. Might as well have some backup.

"That would be a good move," he said, letting her off the hook. The last thing he wanted to do tonight, if things went wrong, was die with any misunderstanding between them. "What about Katherine Fowler?" he inquired. "How is she holding up?" At some point in the past hour Ann had mentioned that she needed to call her.

"She believes we're going to bring her daughter home to her."

Nathan had to see that the lady wasn't disappointed. No matter what else happened, he had to get those children back home to their families. He couldn't let those children down and he couldn't let Ann down. Somehow in the past forty-eight hours she had come to mean far more to him than was logical.

But on some level he understood that logic wasn't a part of this thing happening between them.

"So..." Ann searched his face, his eyes, as if worried that he might be keeping something from her. "What can we do between now and nine?"

"We wait."

It wasn't the answer she'd wanted any more than it was the one he'd wanted to give. But it was the only option they had...for now.

Chapter Eighteen

5:30 p.m.

"This is your chance to redeem yourself, Owen."

Owen kept the smile pinned in place despite the worry churning inside him.

He didn't want to do this.

It was way too dangerous. He hadn't hired on to deliver money to mercenaries. Not one like Damon Savoy. The man was crazy. A genius but crazy as a loon. He would trade, sell or kill his own mother if the price was right.

"The job is very simple, Owen," Kendall went on as if sensing his uncertainty. "You stand by with the money and his people will return the children to the warehouse. The task will be over and done with in mere minutes."

As long as *he* didn't end up dead, Owen wanted

to toss back at this uncaring boss. Kendall wouldn't care if he ended up dead any more than he'd cared about those two men who had been watching the children.

This had gone too far. Way too far.

Just maybe what Owen needed was some insurance.

He had made up his mind. Kendall had gone around the bend. Lost his mind. Dropped over the edge. This whole scheme was out of control and he just wouldn't let it go. The man was nuts!

Owen understood how these things worked. If Kendall's actions were discovered, he would blame everything on Owen. Owen had done all the legwork for him. Made calls, deliveries. Everything. He was the only connection from Kendall to the children to the scuzzball mercenaries Kendall had hired to get the job done. Owen would be the one blamed if this thing blew up in their faces.

But not if he made his move first.

"I won't let you down, Mr. Kendall," Owen assured him. "I will make sure nothing goes wrong this time."

Kendall smiled. His posture visibly relaxed. "Excellent. I knew I could count on you, Owen." He retrieved a briefcase from beneath his desk, placed it flat on the top and opened it to show the stacks of pristine bills. "I need those children, Owen. I know now what will hurt him more than anything else."

Him. The Guardian Angel. Nathan Tyler. He was going to meet with Kendall in just over three hours.

Kendall's words filtered through Owen's churning thoughts. "You're releasing the children so that he'll turn himself over to you," Owen said, more to make sure the plan hadn't changed than to question his boss's thinking.

Another of those sadistic smiles slid across Kendall's face. "The children are the only way I can make him feel the pain I need him to feel," Kendall countered. "I want him to watch them die, one by one. Then he'll die."

Owen forced the properly impressed expression and nodded knowingly. But inside, where no one else could see, he was screaming.

Kendall was going to kill the children.

He'd sworn that none of the children would be harmed. That this was about vengeance for his son's death.

Owen had to do something.

He could not be a part of this…not anymore.

Chapter Nineteen

"I don't like this strategy." Ann shook her head as she considered the map of the Baltimore tourist hot spot known as the Power Plant Live! By nine the indoor-outdoor party-central locale would be jam-packed. Dozens of restaurants and bars, live concerts. Too crowded, period.

They had received the location ten minutes ago, with only ninety minutes left until the rendezvous time. This was just another trap. One, she felt too damned confident, he wouldn't be walking away from.

Who was she kidding? The deal was he would trade himself for the remaining four children.

Ian Michaels and Simon Ruhl were standing by, prepared to help in any way possible. The Bureau, as well as Victoria's research department, was running down every conceivable lead on Damon Savoy. He was like a damn phantom.

Like the man whose life she feared for at that very moment.

"This is the way it has to go down," he reminded her when she was all too well aware of how it had to happen.

He was right, but that didn't mean she had to like it.

"You and your colleagues are not to move in until the children have been released," he said for the nth time.

"Anything could happen during those seconds or minutes required for confirmation."

The children were supposed to be released to her at the main entrance the moment Nathan was in the unsub's custody.

No matter the lengths they attempted to find this man named Savoy, Ann was certain—dead certain—he was not the one orchestrating this nightmare. He was just the go-to man to get the job done. A criminal for hire.

But if they could find Savoy and get a lead on where the children were being held, then they could avoid this showdown altogether.

Even as hope sprouted at the idea, the minutes

passing way too fast mocked her. They were running out of time in one hell of a hurry.

"There's no one else—" she fixed her gaze on his "—who wants you dead?" And that was what this was about.

They had considered every family member or close friend of victims the Guardian Angel had left in his wake and had come up empty-handed. The Bureau hadn't had any better luck.

There simply wasn't anyone at which to point.

And yet someone wanted him badly enough to host this entire event, including the abduction of six children. Had the abductions simply been a way to get his attention, to lure him into the game? Or had tonight been the planned endgame all along?

Ann's cell phone vibrated. She slid it out of her pocket, her pulse hammering at the idea that this could be good news—at the very least, beneficial news.

"Martin."

"Ms. Ann Martin?"

Male. Not a voice she recognized.

"Yes, this is Ann Martin." Her senses shifted into a different gear, this one cautionary.

"You don't know me," the man said, "but I have information that could help you."

Initial analysis: he sounded nervous, tense.

"I'm always appreciative of helpful information, Mr....?" She left the statement dangling to see if he intended to give his name.

"I know where the children will be in less than one hour."

Her eyes locked with Nathan's and she motioned for him to come closer. "Sir, if you have any information about the children, I would sincerely appreciate your help." She struggled to control her response, to not spook him.

She wished for a trace, for a miracle. Anything that could put her at this guy's location.

"There's a warehouse on Merchant Drive—"

"There are a lot of warehouses on Merchant Drive," she interrupted so calmly she surprised even herself.

Silence.

Fear hurdled through her. She shouldn't have cut him off.

Nathan touched her arm, the reassuring feel of his fingers on her skin giving her the courage to hold on...to hope.

"Fifteen fifty-five. My car will be parked on the street." He described his car, color, model, year.

Nathan quickly wrote a note that read, *Ask him why?*

Ann moistened her lips and reached for the

courage she'd always been able to count on before. "Why are you doing this? We already have a meeting in—" she glanced at the wall clock "—just under two hours."

"The children won't be at the Power Plant."

The blood rushed through her veins as adrenaline blasted her.

"Do you have any proof of what you're telling me, Mr.…?"

More of that heart-pounding silence.

"My name is Owen Johnson. I work for Phillip Kendall. He is the man you're looking for. He hired a mercenary named Damon Savoy to take the children. Savoy kept the ransoms but wasn't pleased when he didn't get his promised bonus."

Ann wrote the names, circled Kendall's and passed the note to Nathan.

"Why is Mr. Kendall doing this?"

"We could discuss the subject all night, Ms. Martin, but I have to meet Mr. Savoy in approximately forty minutes with the two-million-dollar bonus he was promised. You see, he has the four remaining children. If he doesn't get the money on time, he's going to kill the children."

"I'm on my way, Mr. Johnson." She would need Ian and Simon for this.

"Have your friend Special Agent Lewis come,

as well," Johnson suggested. "I want immunity. Without my help, those children will die."

"I'll call Agent Lewis en route," she promised. "Ms. Martin?"

Ann drew in an unsteady breath of anticipation. "Yes?"

"I'm doing the right thing. Don't make me…or the children…regret it."

The call ended.

Ann entered Ian's cell phone number. "Stand by, Ian, I'm going to tie you in with Special Agent Frank Lewis." When she'd accomplished the three-way call and put it on speaker, Ann quickly summarized the information she had just received. They couldn't keep the Bureau out of the loop any longer.

Nathan didn't look particularly happy, but he knew they couldn't do this alone. They were beyond that point now. Saving those children had to be top priority. Nathan had already located photos of both Phillip Kendall and Owen Johnson and transmitted them to Ian, Simon and Lewis.

"We need to organize SWAT and get into place," Lewis offered.

"There's not time," Nathan argued. "We have to leave now. I can go after Kendall alone. The rest of you should focus on the location where the children will be handed over."

"I don't agree," Ann argued. "Simon, you could provide backup for Nathan."

"I was just thinking that would be a workable solution," Simon agreed. "However, like Nathan said, we need to get moving now. We're going to be cutting this damn close."

"Don't get too close to me," Nathan warned. "Kendall was very specific about what he would do if I didn't show up alone."

Simon suggested, "We can discuss specifics en route."

The call ended. Lewis and Ian would rendezvous with Ann two blocks from the warehouse. Lewis was going to attempt pulling in SWAT for the warehouse location. What went down at Power Plant Live! was pretty much going to be Simon's and Nathan's problem. If anyone other than the usual security showed up at that tourist spot, there could be hysteria. That was the last thing they needed.

Ann gathered her phone, purse and weapon, then followed Nathan to the garage. He tossed her a set of keys that went to a sporty sedan.

This was where they said goodbye.

Maybe for the last time.

The first time, too, actually.

They'd been together pretty much since they'd met.

She didn't want him to do this without her.

"Be very careful," he urged.

She closed her eyes and shook her head. "It's not me I'm worried about." She searched his face then. "The risk is to you."

There wasn't time for any more talk. He kissed her. Long and deep, making her knees go weak.

Then he drew back just far enough to whisper, "Just remember to keep looking forward…no more looking back."

With that, he climbed into his SUV and the garage door went up. She watched as he backed out of the garage and drove through the gate.

He was gone.

Just like that.

Ann scooted behind the wheel of the car and started the engine. It wasn't until she went to shove the hair behind her ear that she realized she was crying.

Damn it.

She refused to allow this to end badly.

Then she prayed. Prayed that God would protect the children…and their Guardian Angel.

THE WAREHOUSE ON Merchant Drive was still dark.

Owen Johnson had not arrived, and it was ten minutes past the agreed-upon time.

"Ann." Agent Lewis leaned forward to speak to her through the bucket seats of the SUV Ian had rented. "If this is some sort of ruse—"

Ann ignored him and looked to Ian. "Any word from Simon?"

Ian shook his head.

Damn it.

Nathan and Simon had arrived at the Power Plant and then Nathan had vanished.

On purpose. She was certain. He wasn't taking any chances with the children.

And, damn it—she pounded the steering wheel with her fist—that just made her respect him more.

He would sacrifice his life for those kids.

"I'm going to have my agents move in at the Power Plant," Lewis informed her, his suspicion rising more and more with each passing second.

"Lewis." Ann grabbed him by the arm when he withdrew his cell phone. "Give this Johnson guy ten more minutes. If Simon can't find Nathan, your men won't be able to, either. The last thing we need is for a show of force to appear in the crowd."

For two, then three frantic beats of her heart she wasn't sure her plea was going to get through. Then he put the phone away.

"Ten more minutes. That's all."

That was all she could ask for.

Headlights appeared in the distance.

Anticipation whirred along Ann's nerve endings. This had to be him.

The car fitting the description Johnson had given eased to the curb across the street from where Ian had parked the SUV. The driver's-side door opened and a short, thin man emerged. He carried a briefcase.

Ann only got a glimpse of his face in the car's interior light, but she was certain it was him.

"That's him," Ian said, confirming her conclusion.

Maybe now they could at least see that the children were ushered to safety.

Ann forced her mind off Nathan and on this phase of the operation. She had to make sure those children were safely returned to their parents.

Katherine Fowler was counting on her.

"Ms. Martin?"

She recognized the unsteady voice as that of the man who had called her claiming to be Owen Johnson.

"Yes." She met him in the middle of the street.

"I had some difficulty getting away. We have to hurry," he urged. "Savoy will be here any minute. The three of you need to get out of sight before he arrives." He glanced at the SUV. "Perhaps you could move the SUV farther down the block."

Ian reached for the keys. "I'll take care of that and meet you inside."

"Use the entrance on the east side," Johnson said as he started toward the warehouse.

Ann and Lewis followed.

As they entered the dark building, Johnson demanded, "Do you have my immunity papers?"

Ann wasn't even going to attempt explaining that one to the man. Lewis could deal with it.

Inside, Johnson flipped on a series of switches that flooded the easternmost part of the warehouse with light. Electronic equipment was stacked two stories high in most of the open space she could see.

"We have the attorney general's office working on that right now," Lewis assured in answer to his inquiry. "But you have my word," he added, "that if those children are returned safely, you will have full immunity."

Johnson hesitated, seemed to ponder if he still wanted to do this, then said, "All right, but—" he turned to Ann "—you're my witness. He said I would have full immunity if the children were returned safely."

"Agreed," Ann confirmed. "Can we get down to business, please? You expect Savoy any minute?"

"Yes." He patted the briefcase. "I have his bonus. He's to bring the children here." Johnson smiled. "You needn't worry. He will be here."

"What are your instructions once you have the children in your custody?" Lewis asked him.

Ian rejoined them just then.

"I was to take them to Mr. Kendall."

"So you know where he's planning to take Guardian Angel?"

Ann hadn't considered that Johnson would have that information, though she well should have.

"You mean Nathan Tyler?" He looked smug. "Yes, I know where he will be."

"Was it ever in the plan to release the children?" She had to ask. She was getting a very bad feeling about this whole situation.

Owen Johnson visibly paled. "I…I believe Kendall intended to kill them as a way of punishing Tyler."

Ann's throat closed. A man who wouldn't think twice about killing a child sure as hell wouldn't blink at killing another man.

Any hope she'd held out for Nathan's safe escape evaporated.

Johnson looked at his watch. "He should have been here by now."

His cell phone issued a warning that Johnson had an incoming call. He fished the phone from his jacket pocket and checked the caller ID display.

"It's about time." He opened the phone. "Johnson." He listened a moment. "Come in the front entrance. I have what you want."

Ann faded into the shadows, remaining as close to Johnson as possible. Ian and Lewis took cover out of visual range. There could be no mistakes.

Savoy's long strides as he entered the warehouse put Ann further on edge. A man who knew what he wanted and took it. He owned the world.

Then again, she reasoned, for a man so smart, he certainly had walked into a fairly elementary trap.

"You have the money?" Savoy asked, his tone brisk, pointed.

"Yes." Johnson held on to the briefcase as if he were having second thoughts. "Where are the children?"

"Let me see the money," Savoy commanded.

Not a nice man. Ann didn't have to see or hear more.

Johnson heaved a sigh before placing the briefcase on the nearest level space. He opened the case and gestured for Savoy to have a look.

When the man was satisfied, he said, "Very good."

Ann wanted desperately to reach out and grab the bastard, force him to tell her what he knew.

"I'll call my man and authorize the release of the children."

Johnson frowned as the man dug out his phone. "Wait. I thought you were bringing them here."

Savoy pecked in one number and then the next. "There was a last-minute change of plan. Didn't your employer tell you?"

Johnson held on to the money. "What the hell are you talking about?"

"Call your boss," Savoy suggested. "He asked that the kids be delivered directly to him."

Ann knew what that meant.

"Now give me the money and I'll make the call."

Johnson closed the case and thrust the money at him. As long as he knew where the children were, there was a question about whether or not he could be persuaded to cooperate.

No unnecessary chances. Just do the right thing.

Savoy began entering numbers again.

That was when Ann made her appearance. She stepped out of the shadows, the forty-caliber aimed center chest.

"If I were you, I'd rethink my strategy."

Savoy put his hands up. "What the hell is this?"

Ian Michaels joined them then. He smiled vaguely as he pressed the muzzle of his weapon to Savoy's forehead. "This," Ian said in a tone that could only be called lethal, "is your farewell party, because you're going away for a very, very long time."

Chapter Twenty

It took four men to strap Nathan into the chair, but they got the job done.

He ignored the pain of the beating he'd taken.

"Now that's more like it." Phillip Kendall stood over Nathan, smiling as if he'd just discovered the cure for cancer. "You may wait outside," he ordered the four hirelings waiting nearby.

Nathan supposed things would get interesting now. Not that he was looking forward to the pain, but he was more than ready to know what this man wanted. He didn't know Kendall. Had never had any contact with him, personal or professional.

Strange that his life would end this way, in the hands of a stranger. But at least he would die for something—the lives of four children.

The children would be safe. Ann would be safe. Rescuing those children meant as much to her as it did to him. He was glad he could help accomplish that result. He was glad he'd had the chance to know her, if only for a little while.

"I've waited more than a year to meet you," Kendall said, luring Nathan's attention back to the here and now. "I've looked forward to this moment more than you can possibly comprehend."

Nathan wasn't sure of the drug he'd been given once he'd been strapped into the chair. Something by injection. Maybe a tranquilizer since he felt tired and his limbs had grown heavy. Whatever it was, he would fight the effects as long as possible. The one last thing he wanted before he died was answers.

"In case you're wondering," Kendall said as if Nathan had said the last out loud, "you were given a muscle relaxer. Something to ensure your cooperation for just a little while. You'll stay fully conscious until I decide otherwise."

"What do you want from me, Kendall?" Might as well get that part out of the way.

"You rescued a little boy last year," Kendall said as he walked around Nathan's secured position. "Thomas Mitchell."

Nathan remembered. The boy had been missing for two weeks. He'd been sexually abused and drugged by his kidnappers. The bastards responsible had tried to kill the boy before Nathan could get to him. Nathan had arrived in the nick of time. He'd had to kill both of his captors to save the child.

"I remember," Nathan said. If there had been a connection between Kendall and the child or either of the scumbags who'd hurt him, Nathan hadn't found it during his recent search for motive.

Kendall moved momentarily out of visual range, then returned pushing a stainless-steel cart. He parked it next to Nathan's chair. The cart held an array of torture instruments. Clamps, scalpels, forceps, a little something to administer shock treatments. Oh, yeah, lots of fun party favorites.

"One of the men you killed was Ken Phillips," Kendall told him. "Just a boy himself."

"Twenty-two," Nathan said. "Dark hair and eyes." His gaze locked with Kendall's. Nathan never forgot the faces of the men or women he was forced to kill. *"He died first."*

Kendall grabbed a scalpel and inspected it for a moment. "Yes, I'm aware of the order in which the two died." He turned abruptly, swiping Nathan's left cheek with the razor-sharp edge.

Nathan gritted his teeth, refused to cry out in pain. He was well aware that this was what Kendall wanted—to hear his suffering. To relish the sounds of it. Too bad. He wasn't giving him that.

"Think about it," Kendall snarled. "Ken Phillips. Phillip Kendall." He put his face in Nathan's. "He was my son, you animal. You killed my son!"

Well that definitely explained the lengths Kendall had gone to in order to lure Nathan into this game. A rich, powerful man such as himself would do most anything to avenge the death of a loved one. Nathan didn't care what the man did to him…as long as the children were safe.

Kendall took a minute to wire up Nathan. He explained as he did so, "I'm placing each electrode near a specific nerve center where the most pain will be generated. The body is an amazing map of sensors."

"Do you know what your son was doing?" Nathan hadn't meant to ask the question, but there it was, on the table now. Kendall had his agenda; nothing Nathan said or proved was going to change his plan.

"I didn't even know he existed until a few months before I found him," Kendall said as if he hadn't heard the question. "His mother kept him hidden from me. Then she died and he sought me out."

Too bad for him. "Your son should have left the

little boys alone," Nathan told him flatly, stating a fact. "He got as good as he deserved."

Kendall clamped his hand over Nathan's face to shut him up. Pain seared in his jaw. Blood oozed down his neck from the laceration Kendall inflicted.

"Don't speak of him that way," Kendall snarled. "You don't know anything about him."

His hand fell away from Nathan's face and he fixed the final electrode into place. "You see, Mr. *Guardian Angel,*" he said, "my son was innocent."

"That's what the next of kin always says," Nathan argued as he braced for Kendall's response as well as the coming pain.

"No." Kendall placed his hands on the arms of the chair and leaned in nose to nose with Nathan. "You don't understand. My son was going there to rescue the boy, not to harm him. He'd found out the boy was being held there and he wanted to set him free."

That statement gave Nathan pause. He played the scene from that night over in his head. Something was off, but nothing nearly so earth-shattering as that. The struggle between him and the two men on the scene had been real, a fight to the death.

"Sometimes we don't like what we learn about

our loved ones, especially after a violent death," Nathan warned. Ken Phillips had fought Nathan hard. "If your son had been innocent, he wouldn't have tried to stop me from freeing the child."

Kendall moved his head from side to side. "He was trying to free the child and protect me."

Arguing with the man was pointless. "Believe what you will, but your son had a fetish for young boys."

Kendall laughed, but the sound held no humor. "Fool. The fetish was *mine*."

Shock radiated through Nathan. Had he killed the wrong man?

"I was the one who took the boy...who enjoyed his young, tender body...not my son!" Kendall sneered. "How does it feel, *Guardian Angel,* to know you made a mistake? You killed the wrong man! What kind of hero does that make you?"

Fury roared through Nathan. Rage that he had killed the wrong man, that this sick bastard was still alive, flowed like fire through his veins.

"Then his death is on you," Nathan said softly, the truth in his words carrying the power. "*You* killed him."

Kendall stepped back and prepared to send a few volts through Nathan's body. He tensed in anticipation of the pain.

Then Kendall tossed the control back onto the cart. “No, I don’t think I’ll go that route.”

Worry gnawed at Nathan. The abrupt shift in demeanor didn’t feel right. What was this piece of crap up to?

“It took me a long time to figure out how to lure you out of seclusion. And even when I had the chance to kill you, I waited.” Kendall smiled triumphantly. “I didn’t want you to simply die from a bullet to the head or a prolonged beating. I wanted to be sure I knew what would really hurt you, what would really make you suffer. And I finally realized what it would take.”

Fear tightened like a noose around Nathan’s throat.

Kendall crossed to the door and opened it. “Bring them in,” he said, still beaming a sick smile in Nathan’s direction.

Four small children were ushered into the room, all shaking and sobbing. Nathan recognized them: the final four of the Fear Factor case.

“You said you would release them,” he protested, his voice cold and weak at the idea of what could happen next. His heart thrashed in his chest. Damn this sick bastard straight to hell!

Kendall’s sadistic smile broadened into a satisfied grin. “I lied.”

Kendall turned back to the cohort who had ushered the children into the room. “Prepare them.” Then he leaned back down to get in Nathan’s face. “I’m going to skin each one of them alive and let you watch. And when they’re all good and dead, I’m going to kill you.” He grinned. “You’ll be begging to die by then.”

Nathan couldn’t let this happen. “There’s just one thing,” he said quietly.

Kendall scoffed. “What could you possibly have to say that I would care to hear?”

“Something your son told me as I was cutting off the flow of air to his lungs.”

Kendall put his face right in Nathan’s. “Shut up, you son of a bitch!”

“Come on,” Nathan urged. “Don’t you want to hear what his last words were?”

Kendall stilled, his expression suddenly expectant. Nathan leaned his face forward as if he intended to whisper in the man’s ear.

“He said…” Nathan sank his teeth into Kendall’s neck as deep and as hard as he could—right where the carotid artery lay. Blood spurted. Kendall reeled back, screaming. His hands flew to this throat, but it was too late. Blood spewed between his fingers, gushed down his chest. Two more of his men rushed into the room. The children screamed.

Nathan spat the taste of blood and flesh from his mouth. Struggled to free himself from the chair.

One of Kendall's cohorts stabbed Nathan with something that felt like a needle. Another leveled a bead on Nathan with his handgun, right between the eyes.

An explosion rent the air.

The bastard dropped to the floor right next to Kendall.

"Nobody move!" the man who'd fired his weapon shouted as he barged fully into the room.

SWAT. Nathan recognized Special Agent Lewis.

And then...Ann.

She rushed to Nathan. Her hands shook as she struggled to release him.

"Help me get him loose!" she shouted at anyone listening.

The muscle relaxer seemed to kick in at that moment. Nathan's head started to swim and his consciousness faded a little.

Wait...he couldn't feel his body anymore.

And then the room went black.

NATHAN AWOKE slowly. The taste in his mouth was bitter. He reached out for something to grab on to.

"It's okay."

Soft hands ushered his arm back down to his side. His eyes opened.

Ann.

Thank God. She was here and okay.

"Where…?" He cleared his throat and tried again. "Where am I?" Hell? Prison? He'd expected to end up in one or the other.

"You're at Bay General." She curled her fingers around his hand, cradled it in hers. "You're going to be fine."

The muscle relaxer. "What did Kendall give me?"

Ann's eyes glistened with emotion. "The muscle relaxer was administered in a lethal dose."

Damn. Kendall's hireling must have injected him with more of the muscle relaxer when Nathan had felt that stab with the needle.

"The children?" His eyes searched hers. "They're okay?" If the children were safe, he might just be able to live with himself after this. If not…

She nodded, the emotion winning the battle she waged. "They're all fine. Back home with their families." Tears slid down her soft cheeks.

He let go a big breath, reached up and traced the soggy path. "Good."

The next part of his nightmare bobbed to the surface of his hazy thoughts. He was most likely in custody even as he lay here.

"What about Lewis?"

Nathan wasn't looking forward to a trial…or to the possibility of prison. But that was what expensive attorneys were for. He was not ashamed of what he had done to save all those children. He'd only been doing what had to be done. The world needed to wake up to the problem of child abuse, especially sexual predators. He intended to continue doing all that he could do—financially and otherwise. Prison wouldn't stop him.

"That's the funny thing," Ann said, a smile replacing the painful emotions that had clouded her face. "When Agent Lewis wrote his report, he indicated that the Guardian Angel was just an urban legend. No one could really determine if he actually existed. The Bureau's convinced the Guardian Angel is really a group of vigilantes. No one man could do all that Guardian Angel does."

Nathan's dry lips managed to smile. "I'll be damned."

Ann kissed him, softly, sweetly. "All you have to do is get well and go back to being you."

"What about you?" He wrapped his fingers

around her hand, held it close to his heart. He didn't want to lose her. If she returned to her life in Chicago, he might never see her again. "Are you going to go back to being you?"

She nodded firmly. "As a matter of fact, I'm going back to my hometown and set an old record straight. It's way past time that old bastard paid for what he did, and I intend to make it happen."

The wobble in her voice on the end told him that no matter how strong she tried to sound, she was a little afraid—but damn well determined.

Good for her.

He made up his mind then and there. "If you can wait until I'm out of here, I'd really like to go with you." He didn't want her to do this alone.

Her breath caught and then she kissed him again.

"I would love that," she whispered between soft little kisses. "Thank you. Thank you."

"What good is a guardian angel," he whispered against those silky lips of hers, "if he can't be there when you need him?"

She smiled, and what he saw in her eyes made his heart react. He splayed the fingers of his right hand on her neck and pulled her closer. "After that business is taken care of, I think we need a nice, long vacation. Somewhere in the Caribbean, preferably."

He kissed her, lost himself to the incredible sensations of promise.

How had he lived this long without her?

Life was going to be good.

Really good.

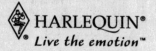

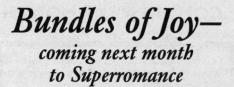

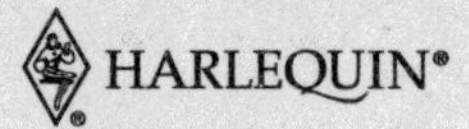

INTRIGUE®

COMING NEXT MONTH

#1047 IN NAME ONLY? by Patricia Rosemoor

The McKenna Legacy

This wasn't Michael Eagan's first high-profile murder case—but it *was* his first McKenna. He'll have to be a good man to charm Flanna, and live dangerously to keep her alive.

#1048 MYSTERIOUS MILLIONAIRE by Cassie Miles

Wealthy adventurer Dylan Crawford is a man of many secrets. So when Elle Norton goes undercover on his estate to investigate a family death, what she discovers about the man is more revealing than she expected.

#1049 WYOMING MANHUNT by Ann Voss Peterson

Thriller

Riding horseback through the Wyoming wilderness was supposed to be the trip of a lifetime for Shanna Clarke—instead she found herself running for her life. Now only rancher Jace Lantry can help her find justice—and exact revenge.

#1050 THE HORSEMAN'S SON by Delores Fossen

Five-Alarm Babies

Collena Drake thought she'd never see her son again after he was stolen at birth. But she found him, in the care of Dylan Greer, a wealthy Texas horse breeder with a dark past. Despite their differences, the two would have to work together to uncover an illegal adoption ring to build their new family.

#1051 AVENGING ANGEL by Alice Sharpe

Elle Medina was the sole survivor of a brutal slaying—and sought to bring down the crime boss that set it off. Undercover DEA agent Pete Waters was tasked with keeping that man alive. At cross purposes, neither knew mercy—in love or death.

#1052 TEXAS-SIZED SECRETS by Elle James

Cattle rustlers, ranch foreclosure and pregnancy were all Texas-sized problems that even Mona Grainger wasn't stubborn enough to think she could handle alone. Enter Reed Bryson, who could ride, rope, kiss… and certainly handle a gun.